THE STARLINGS
& OTHER STORIES
Editor ANN CLEEVES

12 stories inspired by David Wilson photographs
A Murder Squad & Accomplices Anthology

Ann Cleeves, Cath Staincliffe, Chris Simms,
Christine Poulson, Helena Edwards, Jim Kelly, Kate Ellis,
Margaret Murphy, Martin Edwards, Mary Sharratt,
Toby Forward and Valerie Laws.

GRAFFEG

'As a landscape photographer I strive to produce images that will stimulate the viewer and provoke them into interpreting what they see; investing their own narrative into the photograph. For an esteemed group of writers to choose a selection of my images as the inspiration and catalyst for their own stories is a great honour.'

DAVID WILSON

The Starlings & Other Stories published by Graffeg
September 2015 © Copyright Graffeg 2015
ISBN 9781909823747

Images © David Wilson, taken from *Pembrokeshire*
by David Wilson ISBN 9781905582594

Designed and produced by Graffeg www.graffeg.com
Graffeg Limited, 24 Stradey Park Business Centre,
Mwrwg Road, Llangennech, Llanelli, Carmarthenshire
SA14 8YP Wales UK Tel 01554 824000 www.graffeg.com

Graffeg are hereby identified as the authors of this work
in accordance with section 77 of the Copyrights, Designs
and Patents Act 1988.

A CIP Catalogue record for this book is available from
the British Library.

CONTENTS

Foreword	4
Homecoming Cath Staincliffe	6
Sirens Mary Sharratt	18
The Wizard's Place Chris Simms	38
The Man Who Didn't Breathe Jim Kelly	56
The Starlings Ann Cleeves	72
Mountains Out of Molehills Valerie Laws	88
Port Lion Margaret Murphy	106
Sorted Toby Forward	116
Through the Mist Martin Edwards	136
House Guest Helena Edwards	164
Secrets Kate Ellis	180
Weeping Queens Christine Poulson	204
Author biographies	222

FOREWORD
MURDER SQUAD

Crime writers are obsessed by darkness and light. In our novels, the shadier side of human nature holds sway for a while: individuals do terrible things, groups surrender to base urges, communities are complicit in shocking acts. But this blackness doesn't last. The detective gets his man, the victim fights back, the downtrodden turn the tables. Justice shines through.

So when we received a proposal that involved writing short stories based on black and white photographs, we were intrigued. What sort of photographs? Were the images urban? Journalistic? Portraits? None of these things, it turned out. They were landscapes. And all from one very rural location: Pembrokeshire.

Murder Squad was formed in the year 2000. The idea of Margaret Murphy, it originally involved several crime writers who were keen to promote their work in person – be it in libraries and bookshops or at literature festivals and crime writing conferences. Since then careers have evolved. Many nominations have been received and several awards have been won – national and international. Some of them specifically for short stories. There have even been a few TV series created. Murder Squad now consists of six writers: Margaret Murphy,

Ann Cleeves, Cath Staincliffe, Martin Edwards, Kate Ellis and Chris Simms.

As luck would have it, each of us is familiar with this stunning part of Wales – through leisurely childhood holidays or snatched weekends away. When we got to view David Wilson's work, the sense of excitement was instant. These weren't the cosy compositions of tourist shop tea-towels. The images were starkly arresting. By his own admission, David's photographs – beautiful as they are – often carry 'a sense of eerie foreboding'. Brooding woods emerge from pale mist. Lonely farmsteads are threatened by stormy skies. Troubled seas lunge violently at the shore. Even when the natural elements are at peace, the photographs have dramatic power. An abandoned building leaves you wondering what happened to those who once lived there. Did that solitary boat lying out on the mudflats run aground under the cover of night? What things has that sentinel-like stone witnessed, standing as it has for countless centuries...

Reactions from Murder Squad members included the words 'bewitching', 'enchanting' and 'haunting'. Each photograph 'seemed to whisper of stories aching to be told'. To ensure there would be enough of these stories for a reader to enjoy, we all invited one other author to contribute – an associate Murder Squad member, or accomplice, if you like. The twelve of us each chose an image. Then we went away promising that, several months down the line, we'd return with a short story influenced by crime. The result is this anthology, *The Starlings & Other Stories*.

It's been fun. And we hope that what we've written captures some of the mystery and magic that made David's photographs such an inspiration for us all.

Chris Simms

HOMECOMING

CATH STAINCLIFFE

The day was ending as he reached the house.

The roof still held but the windows had gone, the doors too. And in front where the path had once been, a cloud of gnats danced over a large puddle. A few more years and the whole lot would collapse, the stone return to the earth, the foundations become choked by rough grass and bracken and briars.

'I had a little nut tree, nothing would it bear, but a silver nutmeg and a golden pear.'

He hadn't thought of the song for years. Susan singing. Whirling round in the snow, her new purple herringbone coat, the colour of the heather on the moor, flecked with white and black, spinning out as she turned. Her raven hair whipping about. Always dancing, like she couldn't keep still. She would learn the latest moves in the playground and teach Hugh.

'Giddy goat,' their father would say, smiling.

But their mother called her wilful and impudent.

'This dump,' Susan used to call it, 'I'm going to leave this dump and go to London.' She would be a dancer or a singer. Hugh didn't want her to go and leave him behind but she promised to send for him.

'We could share a flat.'

'And have parties.'

'And go travelling in a bus with all our friends.'

'And never go to chapel again.'

The chapel, Mother's passion, dominated their lives. Mother had come to Wales as an evacuee from Liverpool. Her family were killed in the Blitz and so she had stayed on with the old minister and his housekeeper. He was of the fire and brimstone school and taught Mother his ways. Hugh remembered her voice, going on and on and on about the wickedness of people, how corrupt and immoral they were, perverted and shameless, degenerates living in the gutter. On and on until Father would get up and walk out. He'd be gone for hours. And Hugh would have a sick ache inside of him in case Father didn't come home but he always did.

Hugh stepped inside the cottage. The place was stripped bare, he wondered who'd done that, removed beds and the dresser, the table and chairs. It smelled of mice and mould. The paint on the walls was mottled and flaking, chunks of plaster littered the floor. In the back room were signs that people had sheltered here: old fires, cans and crisp packets. Tramps, perhaps, too far off the beaten track for anyone else.

Out the back, wilderness had taken over. He walked, treading down brambles thick as rope, the fruit on them glistening fat and black. Glass and guttering snapping underfoot. This was a kitchen garden once, the soil was poor but his mother had coaxed potatoes and leeks, raspberries and peas from it.

The hazel tree was still there at the end beside the hawthorn. He and Susan would pick the cobnuts, once the bright green shells turned brown, cracking them in their back teeth and fishing out the sweet nut meat.

Hugh loved Susan, she was the warmth of the house, so when she went off to Cardiff he had for a time resented her. He wondered if she would send for him once he was finished with school. But no word came and eventually he took up the apprenticeship in the Merchant Navy.

He'd sent a postcard or two at first, from new continents, new countries, out of a sense of duty. He wrote, once he was settled in New

Zealand, so they'd have an address for him, but got no reply.

Forty-seven years since he had left. Nearly half a century.

His mother posted a note, brief and formal, in 2001, after his father's funeral. And once she'd gone, the solicitor had written to say the cottage, with its two acres, was his. Nothing left to Susan, all to him.

Let it rot, he thought, but then he got the diagnosis. The only treatment palliative. He needed to put his affairs in order while they'd still let him travel. Straightforward enough in Auckland: no dependents, no property to dispose of. Raymond and he had built a life together but Raymond had died far too young – before they'd developed the antiretrovirals – and Hugh had never found anyone else. He would leave his savings to Susan and the same with the cottage, it wasn't worth much but it would be hers. After floundering himself, he'd hired an investigator to trace her. No news as yet. According to the records she'd not married but Hugh took heart from the fact that she hadn't died either.

Hugh looked across the moorland to the horizon. You could see for fifteen miles, and no other building in view. Rushes marked the paths of streams descending the hills from the limestone crags, and here and there were lone trees forced to grow sideways by the wind. Sheep dotted the landscape, and lower down the valley the slopes were divided by dry-stone walls. None of it had changed.

He was eleven when Susan fell pregnant. She was fifteen. She never went back to school after Christmas, she had to stay in: no chapel, no trips to town. Hidden if anyone called, though barely anyone ever did. Glandular fever, that's what Hugh had to say if he was asked. She had told him about Gwyn Davies, in the year above her, how he was sweet on Susan, how he wanted to go to London too. She swore Hugh to silence.

He knew it was a terrible thing, a sin. An abomination, his mother called it, one of the few times she mentioned the fact. It was a secret. Even in the house, between the four of them, it was a secret. Everybody pretending that it wasn't there, wasn't happening. When the time came the child would go to a decent Christian family, he'd overheard his mother tell Susan.

Susan never talked about the baby. One time Hugh asked: a Sunday when they were alone, their parents at the morning service. Hugh had been sick with tonsillitis, he was almost better but claimed he still felt ill so he could stay behind. They had switched the radio over to the Light Programme, *Easy Beat*. The reception was crackly, Billy J Kramer, Gerry and The Pacemakers, The Beatles, *I Saw Her Standing There*, but Susan sang along and Hugh joined in. He danced too and she cheered him on. Susan was stroking her stomach which was big by then and Hugh said, 'Does it feel strange?' And she'd flinched, like he'd pinched her, and she moved her hand away. He had felt stupid. But then she'd started on knock-knock jokes and he felt better.

It was July, hot and airless, and Hugh had woken in the middle of the night, thirsty, to hear his parents arguing.

'I'll fetch the doctor—' his father said.

'No,' his mother said.

'If we call the hospital—'

'It's nature's way,' she said.

'It's too soon,' his father said.

'Do you want us shamed, vilified? Do you want the whole valley to know we have a daughter who's no better than a bitch in heat?' his mother said.

'But if—'

'It's God's will,' she said, 'and nature's way.'

'Jean—'

'No.'

Hugh heard steps, the creak of boards by Susan's door.

'Leave her,' Mother said, 'I'll see to her.'

The front door shut, and then there was the bang of the gate as his father left.

Susan was moaning.

When it got light Hugh had to stay outside all day, weeding the vegetable patch, which was full of couch grass and dock and thistle.

His mother called Hugh for tea. Just the two of them at the table. 'Your sister is ill, so you leave her alone, you hear?' she said.

'Yes,' he said, 'Is it the baby coming?'

'There is no baby,' his mother said.

And later still, as the dusk came in, his father was back.

Hugh heard him digging, the crisp cut of the spade, the chink when it struck rock. Peering out of his bedroom window, Hugh saw his father with the spade, at the end of the vegetable beds, along from the hazel tree.

Susan never sang again, not that he heard. She was sullen, refusing to speak, not eating or washing, her face to the wall. Now and then exploding with an anger that seemed too large for the house. Shouting and swearing, calling his mother awful names and hitting out. Raving that if Mother had sent for help the baby might have lived, that she was no better than a murderer. His mother would slap her quiet. And if Susan still ranted his mother would reach for the stick.

Hugh had been camping with the scouts in August, a brief respite. His father collected him from the hall in town after finishing his shift at the quarry. He told Hugh on the drive back that Susan had run away. That Mother was furious but there was nothing to be done about it.

Hugh was cross too, that she'd gone without telling him.

'Did she go to London?' Hugh said.

'I don't know,' his father said, 'Cardiff probably.'

When he got the chance, Hugh sneaked into her room to check, and it was true. Her coat and bag were gone. She'd not even left a note for him but then if Mother had discovered the note she might have found a way to stop Susan going.

Hugh waited for news, a letter, but none came. Or if it did, his mother got to it first and threw it on the fire.

Word got round school that Susan had gone to Cardiff. Boys would come up to him saying, 'Your sister's working the docks, isn't she?' Sniggering. He puzzled over that, a fifteen-year-old girl hired as a stevedore, until Thomas Vaughan told him, in the crudest possible terms, how she was earning a living. Hugh's face burned up and he wanted to thump Thomas Vaughan but he just walked off. After that, school was a torture to be endured. The days, the months, stretched out, aching into the distance.

The house was a miserable place with Susan gone. Hugh thought his father missed her too, silent on their morning drives when he'd drop Hugh off on the road to walk the rest of the way to school. Silent all the time. Away from the house even more. His father looked older, smaller, like an apple shrinking with age. If Father had only stood up

to Mother then maybe the doctors could have saved the baby and
Susan wouldn't have gone just yet.

As soon as he could, Hugh left it all behind.

Hugh found a stone, almost level, where he could sit and watch the
sun bleed across the sky and sink beyond the horizon.

As the darkness fell, the bats came out to feed, spinning and
swooping not far above his head. Stars glittered and a waxing crescent
moon hung, the other way around from at home.

The pain was back, it was time for his tablets, so he rose slowly
and used the light on his phone to guide his way through the
undergrowth and the shell of the house back to the car where he
would sleep. No doubt the hire company would charge him for the
state of it, mud and scratches from bucking up the old lane.

The temperature soon dropped, his breath misted the windows but
he had a blanket and a flask of coffee so he drank half of it and then
pushed the seat back as far as it would go and pulled the blanket up
to his chin.

He wondered if she had made it to London, had become a singer
or a dancer. If she had any more children. Then he'd be an uncle. That
thought made him feel odd, nice though.

As first light crept over the land, Hugh took his tablets and
finished the coffee. He got the things out of the boot. He had called
at a large DIY store on the new ring road outside of town where
he'd bought the spade and a plastic storage box in case he did find
anything. A bundle of bones he guessed by now. Hugh hoped that
Susan wouldn't think he was acting out of turn, wanting to find
the child and give him a burial, when it was her baby after all. He'd

intended to discuss it with her, plan it together. What if they couldn't track her down? What would he put on the headstone? *Baby born too soon.* Was it a boy or a girl? Had she named the child? He wasn't even sure of the date, he only knew it was July, 1963. It would be so much easier to do all this with her.

The day was fair, a breeze from the west, clear blue sky and the promise of warmth to come. He saw rabbits scatter as he walked to the hazel tree.

The ground was hard to dig, tangled thick with roots and he hadn't the strength that he used to have. He stopped several times, sweat stinging his eyes, blisters breaking on his palms. After half an hour, he'd found nothing. Had he been wrong, guessing his father had buried the stillborn baby? Was his memory playing tricks?

Hugh began again, a new hole further along. The sun burned the back of his neck and he heard the burbling song of skylarks, and grasshoppers cricking, then the whistling cry of a red kite. He straightened up and narrowed his eyes to watch the raptor circling the hillside.

He kept digging. He found a tiny hand first, like a monkey's paw, and then the rest of it, not much bigger than a rabbit's skeleton, along with scraps of fabric, a towel or something. He lifted the bones out and placed them in the plastic box. He thought it was all there but decided to dig another foot to the right to make sure. When his shovel hit resistance, he tested the soil around, driving the spade in until he got purchase, digging it out. Scooping back more earth. Panting, his throat parched.

Herringbone cloth, the colours still clear.

Hanks of black hair.

His blood froze.

Trembling he dug some more and found a skull, a jagged line fractured the temple.

Susan spinning, her arms wide, her voice strong and clear, *'I skipped over water, I danced over sea and all the birds in the air they couldn't catch me.'*

Hugh saw the cotton grass shiver in the wind and heard the song of the skylarks rejoicing above.

He set down his spade and knelt and lifted his face to the sky.

SIRENS
MARY
SHARRATT

I was born with witch's hair, pure blazing red, as shrill as poisonous toadstools. Girls with hair like mine brought bad luck. They caused milk to sour and butter to curdle in the churn. If a seafaring man passed a red-haired maid on the way to his ship, disaster would strike. A storm would brew up and hurl his vessel to the bottom of the ocean where flame-haired mermaids would pick clean his bones.

To save me from my mother's fate, Father bade me to keep my hair tucked carefully away inside my coif. But what I could not hide were my eyes, which saw everything, even in the dark.

Seven is a magic number. Sailors seek to ward off storms by tying their masts in seven knots. The year I turned seven, I still lived with my sister Sarah, seven years older than me, and our father in Ram's Head, a village on the high moors. Sheep slept in the common, their bleats and blurry white shapes haunting the night. Men gathered to drink at The Silent Woman, and on Sunday we squeezed into Saint Stephen's Church to hear the sermons of heaven and hell. When my mind wandered, I looked out the windows at the headstones, but none bore my mother's name. A woman such as her could not be buried in hallowed ground.

Witch-spawn, folk called my sister Sarah and me. Apart from each other, we had no friends. Sarah was the closest thing I ever had to a mother. My real mother I could not remember. Father never spoke of her. He forbade my sister and me to speak of her. It seemed he wanted us to believe that she had never existed, that we had sprung from him alone.

But Sarah remembered. Sometimes she dreamt of Mother and awakened crying. Sometimes in secret, she spoke of her. My sister said so many different things, according to her whims, that I never knew what to believe.

She said, 'Mother was beautiful and kind. She came from Wales where the mountains touch the sea. What people say of her is a parcel of lies.'

She said, 'Our mother was a witch, and witches must hang.'

She said, 'I, too, am a witch.'

I cried and told her such talk was wicked and that Father would thrash her if he heard.

She said, 'Father's little darling, you are. You belong to him. But I belong to her.'

Amongst themselves, the neighbours whispered that Sarah was just like our mother, but out of pity for Father, they did not cry witch. Yet the signs were there for all to see. Though a maid of fourteen, my sister could easily pass as seventeen with her womanly figure. And she knew things no ordinary girl could know. She hungered and thirsted for knowledge. Whenever a pedlar or tinker passed our door, or a local girl came home after a stint of service at the gentry's estate, Sarah would beg and cajole the poor bewildered soul for any scrap of knowledge of the world beyond our village. It was as if she had been planning her escape all along.

Father was a bonesetter, the only one in miles, and the closest thing our village had to a physician. Early one morning he set off for a distant hamlet to attend to a drayman's dislocated jaw.

He hadn't been gone an hour before Sarah opened the chest and took out our mother's cloak, made of such finely woven wool that Father hadn't been able to justify casting it away. Despite the midsummer heat, she tied it over her shoulders and swirled in a circle.

'Come.' She reached for my hand. 'There's something I must show you.'

Our life was so lonely that Sarah was always inventing games for us, but I resolutely kept on carding wool, as Father had bidden me to do. By the time he returned that night, he expected the pile of wool in the corner to be carded, combed, and spun. When he was away, he insisted that we stay safe inside the cottage and not wander about the village where we might come to mischief.

'He'll know if we go out,' I said, trying to ignore the way Sarah's eyes shone gold, then brown, like agates at the bottom of the beck.

She put her arms around me and smiled her most coaxing smile, the one that turned me to butter. 'We'll only be gone a short while, love. I've a surprise for you. A secret. Now come.'

My sister led the way across trackless stretches of moorland. Between the tufts of heather and bracken, the ground was boggy and treacherous, and the earth sucked at my feet as if it wanted nothing better than to swallow my one pair of shoes. Sarah hared off ahead while I floundered. The shrill yellow gorse made me think of someone yelling out a warning, ordering us to turn back. I yearned to run home, only I no longer knew where I was.

At last my sister stopped and waited for me to catch up. Still wearing Mother's heavy cloak, her face glowed with sweat.

'Are you thirsty, love?' Her voice was so gentle that my fear and anger died away. 'Look, Judith. Here's a spring.'

From the mossy rocks sprang ribbons of pure water which I caught in my cupped hands. When I'd drunk my fill, Sarah reached into Mother's cloak and pulled out a hunk of bread. I cried out in amazement that she could conjure bread from the folds of her cloak. But when she broke it in two and handed half to me, I took a bite and tasted that it was the bread we had baked the day before.

'Where are we going?' I demanded. 'What's the secret?'

Sarah kissed my brow. 'Wisht, love. We're nearly there.'

The land curved up and up like a hill I would never see the top of, but as I began to weep from the pain in my calves, the ground levelled and began to slope down, unfurling from our feet in a vast green mantle. Far below the land stopped. The horizon was the dazzling blue of a gentlewoman's gown. Though I had lived my first seven years only seven miles from the sea, I had never before laid eyes upon it.

Sarah smiled triumphantly. 'Mermaids live there. Sea monsters, too.'

At the place where the land met the water, there were more buildings than I'd ever seen. When I shaded my eyes and squinted, I made out church towers and a harbour of tall-masted ships.

'That's Whitby.' Sarah spoke with an authority that reminded me of Father.

The curate at Saint Stephen's spoke of Whitby as a port heaving with godless foreigners and sin, as wretched as Babylon.

'How do you know?' I demanded. 'How did you find the way?'

She smiled slyly. 'Mother showed me.'

'Stop!' I cried, thinking she said it to frighten me.

'Wisht, love. I've been here before.' She lowered her face to mine and stroked my hair. 'When I was only small, she took me. It happened before you were born.'

Far away from Father, she spoke of Mother freely.

'Come.' She took my hand.

I baulked and begged her to take me home, thinking of Father and the way he would shout. Bursting into tears, I swore I wouldn't take another step further from home.

Sarah put her lips to my ear. 'Mother's name was Rebecca.'

I stopped crying, for Rebecca was a pretty name and one I had always loved.

Golden light played in my sister's eyes. 'We've come this far, love. Father will be angry in any case. Shall we not take one look at the sea before we walk home? It's just down these hills.'

Mother's name rang inside my head as I followed Sarah to the sea.

Holding fast to Sarah's hand, I gawped at the wealthy merchants' tall stone houses with ships carved over their doors. We leapt out of the way of coaches and carts, and a girl no older than me shouldered past with a basket of silvery fish. We passed an alehouse with its shutters and doors flung open, drunken laughter drifting out. Soon we reached the pier where we threw back our heads to look at the ships with their masts that rose taller than church steeples and at the bare-breasted mermaids that sprang from the prows. Sarah eyed the sailors climbing the riggings. In the heat they were stripped nearly naked. Some of them had the darkest skin I'd ever seen.

'They're Moors,' Sarah whispered, entranced. 'They've a sultan instead of a king. All manner of spices grow in their country.'

'How do you know?'

Light flashed in my sister's eyes. 'Mother knew such things.'

With each breath, I inhaled the aroma of baking fish from the cookshops along the quay. Telling Sarah of my hunger, I resolved to forgive her for the beating Father would give us if only she could pull bread from Mother's cloak once more. But her pockets were now empty.

'We've no money to buy supper, but I'll get some,' she said. 'Wait here.'

Before I could protest, she slipped away, out of my sight. My eyes filled. Listening to the gulls screech and keen, I wondered if she'd abandoned me. A while later, I spotted her down the pier. She'd removed her coif to let her beautiful chestnut hair stream to her waist. I watched her accost a sailor, take his hand, and cup it in hers, watched her tilt her face to his and smile into his eyes. I crept toward her, then hid behind a barrel and listened until my ears burned.

'The lines of your fate and fortune, sir, are engraved upon your palm. Ah, but you are handsome and full of health! Your life-line is long.'

I craned my head around the barrel to see my sister tracing the inside of the sailor's hand.

'But your love-line!' she exclaimed. 'You shall lose your heart to one from across the water, a dark and beautiful girl. Oh, she'll break your heart! But for a time you'll be so happy. You'll have such bliss as you've never known.'

The sailor grinned and called for his friends. Soon a whole group of them crowded round her and offered her their palms. Greeting them like long lost friends, she promised them wealth, long life, and broken hearts, and they filled her hands with coins, which she dropped into the purse that hung from her waist. Finally the lads went on their way and my sister called to me.

'We shall get our supper, Judith.'

Sarah bought a whole baked fish. We devoured it, spitting out the bones. Stray cats came to rub against our ankles and purr for scraps.

'This salty fish,' my sister said, 'has given me a powerful thirst. Wait here.'

My belly full, I forgot my fear of abandonment and was content to play with the cats until she returned with a tankard of ale.

'We must give it back when it's empty.' She took a swig before passing it to me.

Unlike the small beer we drank at home, this was heady and strong, but it quenched my thirst and left me languid and pleasantly drowsy.

My sister, I thought, had become such a beauty, her lovely hair floating down. When men stopped to talk to her, she was pleasant enough but full of a dignity that set her apart. It was as though she had drawn a magic circle around herself that drew men toward her without letting them too close. But as the midsummer sun began to set, the enchantment wore off, and the faces of strangers no longer seemed so friendly. A sailor with stringy yellow hair closed his fist around Sarah's chin and mashed his lips into hers.

'Away from me!' she spat.

He only laughed. His friends crowded round her, blocking her escape.

'Let her be!' I cried, but I was so little that no one paid me any mind.

'Let her be!' I entreated, saying a silent prayer to God whose face blurred with Father's.

Then the notion crossed my mind that neither Father nor God was going to be of any use to us. While the stringy-haired man was crushing his greasy lips into Sarah's, his friends grabbed her from behind and pinned her arms to her sides.

Witch-spawn, folk called me. What if it were true that wicked blood ran in my veins? Sarah had the powers to find her way across the moors and charm coins from the hands of sailors. What powers ran though me? Ripping off my coif, I whipped out my unlucky red hair for the men to see, whirling it in circles like a mad girl, screaming and spitting.

'In the name of the devil!'

Launching myself at the stringy-haired man, I knocked him off balance and he let go of my sister. He tried to grab me, but I seized his hand and bit until he screamed and I tasted blood. As the circle of men parted, Sarah and I broke free, flying up the back streets and alleyways until, winded and panting, we reached the edge of town. Sarah heaved me over a rough stone wall before she plunged after me. As we lay gasping in the twilit grass and caught our breath, she touched my face.

'Your hair.' She took a lock in her hand, gingerly, as if it would burn her. 'Oh, Judy.' A tremor ran through her voice. Then she gathered her wits, lifted her skirts, and pissed like a mare.

Leaving Sarah to her privy, I wandered deeper into the pasture. At the top of a hillock, a devilish black shape stood against the ruddy western sky. The thing had glowing yellow eyes and curling horns. But I stood my ground as the creature hunkered toward me.

'Be gone,' I commanded, waving my hair that gave me such fearful powers. Indeed I could no longer cover it, having lost my coif in the scuffle with the sailors. 'I'm not afraid of you.'

The ram locked eyes with me, then turned and retreated, whereupon I squatted and pissed as grandly as my sister had done.

Under the rising moon, Sarah led me to a grove at the far end of the pasture.

'No thorns here,' she promised. 'Just elderflower and dog wood.'

The dog roses were delicate and fragrant, giving off a soft white glow. Sarah crawled into the green tunnel and spread Mother's cloak on the ground.

'What if the farmer finds us?' I asked, wriggling in after her.

'Wisht. We'll be gone before sunrise.'

Taking off my shoes, I lay in the centre of the cloak. Sarah curled up beside me and folded the edges to enclose us. 'Mother would have been so proud of you today, love. Such a bold girl you were. You had those men trembling. One day they'll sing songs about you. They'll make you into a siren.'

'Tell me about Mother,' I begged.

'She was beautiful,' said Sarah, 'and proud. She did as she pleased. Father could do nothing to stop her. She was a midwife, but the gossips said she was a sly one. She didn't just help birth babies.' My sister's voice trailed off. 'Why do I say such things to you? You're too young. Sleep, Judy.'

'Tell me,' I pleaded. I wanted to talk of Mother the whole night long.

'She was untrue to Father. You can't understand such things. They all laughed at him. Gave him the cuckold's horns. They said it was the devil's work that she never grew great with child. Between having me and having you, there was not one birth. If any wife or spinster wanted rid of the babe growing inside her, she went to Mam.

'Then one day when I was as old as you are now, she was tending Martha Ward's lying-in. The baby was born blue and cold. Martha caught a terrible fever and raved for all to hear how Mam had killed the baby with her witchcraft. Then others began to mutter about the herbs Mam knew that could loosen a baby from the womb. Even

Mam's lover stepped forward, swearing she had bewitched him and led him astray. Do you understand, Judy?' Sarah gave me no chance to answer. 'No. You understand nothing of this.'

Abruptly, my sister's tone changed. 'Once, before this evil happened, a tinker woman passed through our village. Mam took a liking to her and let her read my palm. She said I'd cross the water and lose my heart to a foreigner.'

'What of Mam?' I persisted, not wanting to hear any stories of tinker women.

'Mam knew they'd come to arrest her.' As my sister spoke, she clung to me as if I were some kind of anchor. 'She took me and ran away across the moors to Whitby. It wasn't safe to go by the road or the packhorse trail. She told me, 'You must always know how to find your own way across the moors.' She taught me how to look to the sun for direction. She said, 'Imagine so much water that it touches the sky. That's the sea calling to us. If you only listen, you'll hear. If you're lost, then close your eyes and feel the sea tugging you like a thread. You've eyes in your head, and you've also eyes inside your heart that can see even further. Remember this and you'll always be able to find your way.'

'And that was how Mam and I reached Whitby. She said we'd visit someone she once knew, a mariner's wife. The lady, so Mam said, would lend us money so we could sail away on one of those ships. But when we went to the fine house, the mariner's wife wasn't there. Then they found us, the men from our village—Thomas Ward and his brothers had tracked us with their dogs all the way over the moors.'

My head filled with shadows that set me shivering, but Sarah was of no comfort since she was shivering so hard herself.

'The constable locked us up, then Father came to fetch me home.

But I clung to her cloak so tightly and wouldn't let go no matter how Father tried to pry my fingers loose. In the end, Mam took it off, and Father carried me off and away, bundled in her cloak and screaming for her.

'I only saw her again, when she went on trial at York. They tried to force me to speak against her, but I wouldn't. They said my silence was proof that she had bewitched me. They made me say the Lord's Prayer, but in front of all those gawping, hateful people, Judy, I couldn't remember the words. The judge said this proved she was guilty and she had to hang. I tried to run to her, but they wouldn't let me near her.'

Sarah wept as though she'd never stop.

'Wisht,' I said, stroking her back. 'Wisht.'

'But they couldn't hang her right away, because she was carrying you, Judy. They said that was the devil's work, too, for how could she suddenly find herself with child just as she was sentenced to hang? She bore you in gaol, and once you were safely out of her womb, she laid her head down and died in her cell so they'd never have the pleasure of stringing her up to feed the crows.'

I writhed at the picture my sister's words painted, of crows tearing at our mother's dead flesh as she hung there like a stoned magpie.

'Father went to fetch you home while I had to wait at home and spin. As I spun, I cursed all the wicked folk who accused her. Then Father came home and placed you in my arms. No wet nurse would take you, so I had to feed you cow's milk, and with you crying every hour, I was too busy to finish my work of cursing the neighbours.'

Sarah was breathless. When I touched her face in the darkness, it felt feverish. She couldn't lie still but kept shifting her weight and stretching out her arms to touch the frail dog roses.

'Her blood runs in us,' Sarah whispered in my ear. 'Her powers, too. Today I saw them in you, Judy. She's close by, even now. On the other side, watching over us.'

Even though my sister meant to console me, her words made my flesh crawl. Surely our mother was not in heaven, but in that other place, too terrible to name. By now I'd heard enough of magical powers, and it wasn't a ghostly mother I wanted but my real father, who loved us deep down and was only harsh because he wanted to protect us.

'I want to go home!' By this time I was sobbing.

'Home!' Sarah spat. 'They hate us there. What will happen to us when Father dies? Who will protect us then? We have no home. We belong on the road like tinkers.'

How could we wander the world without a home, I wondered. Lost and reviled, belonging to no one?

'Don't cry, sweeting,' my sister said at last. 'Tomorrow I'll see you safely home, but then I must go away. I hate every soul in that village.'

Despite my longing for Father, I protested that I could never return without her.

She took my face in her hands. 'You have the powers, Judy. They destroyed her, but she lives in us. Even if I wander the world and you live all your days in Father's house, they'll never be able to separate us.'

'Don't tell lies,' I begged her.

Sarah held me and murmured, 'This is your mother, Judy. We're lying on her bones.'

I felt the earth beneath me, softer than any earth I'd ever lain upon. And I smelled the soft white dog roses that enclosed us. When Sarah kissed me, licking the tears from my face like a mother cat,

I closed my eyes and saw a woman with fiery hair she refused to conceal. She held out her arms and called to me. As my sister held me, I knew it was really Mam moving through her. For the first time in my life, I knew what it was to be held by my mother. I felt so safe and loved that I wept, clinging to her and trembling. She held me steady, soothing my fears, embracing me with a love so fierce, it had overpowered death. All I knew was solace as the dog roses dropped their petals on our wet faces and tangled hair.

At sunrise I jerked awake and looked up through the branches to see the crows circling overhead and caw-caw-cawing as if to warn us.

Shaking Sarah's shoulder, I hissed the word, 'Run.'

But it was too late. Men surrounded us and captured my sister as though she were some wild beast. Though she kicked and cursed, they held her fast. When I tried to bite their hands, one of the men just wrestled me into his arms and hauled me off like a pack of dirty wool. They delivered us to Whitby Gaol.

We were as culpable as thieves caught in daylight, my sister and I. She who had enticed the sailors and taken their money for reading their palms—an act of sorcery, according to the law—and me for carrying on like a bewitched, ungoverned thing.

When they whipped us, we wouldn't give them the satisfaction of hearing us cry. Instead we keened. Even in that prison, we felt the sea tugging on us, calling to us like a mother. We were sirens luring ships onto treacherous rocks. We shrieked with the powers that could raise storms and floods. At last the jug-faced youths wielding the whips went white in the face and stumbled sickly away, for they were mere apprentices to their art and their hearts were not yet hardened.

The prison master himself then bound our hands behind our backs and marched us into a windowless cell full of piss-stinking straw. After he bolted the door, we were left in the pitch black. Was I terrified? I was seven. My hair lit up the darkness, crackling like flame over my bleeding shoulders.

The next morning, we staggered to our feet, dry-mouthed and blinking, as the prison master dragged us into the prison yard. The daylight was so unbearably bright that I recoiled. When the prison master yanked us to a halt, my eyes wrenched fully open to see Father looking at Sarah and me as though we were two apparitions.

'The little one goes free,' the prison master told him, untying my hands. 'But the older one's to be sent to York to stand trial at the next Assizes.'

'No!' I cried.

But no one paid me any mind.

Father started slowly toward Sarah who stood as proudly as she always did, even with her hands bound behind her back and pieces of filthy straw stuck in her hair. She stood not as a defiant girl before our father, but as a woman. Her face seemed to have grown lines overnight. His face as colourless as fog, Father stared at her and said the word he'd not uttered for as long as I'd been alive.

He said, 'Your mother.'

He said, 'Sarah, in God's name, you're her likeness.'

Then he began to weep. He reached out to embrace her, but the prison master dragged him away. 'Take the child home. The wench is going to York.'

Father pleaded. He shouted. He tried to bribe the prison master who had already pocketed the sailors' coins from my sister's purse.

Unmoved, the prison master summoned his apprentices to take Sarah back to her cell. Hurling myself at her, I sank my fingers into her cloak and swore I'd never leave her, swore it in our mother's name.

Sarah kicked me away, screaming, 'Are you mad? Go with Father!'

By the time Father brought me home, a mighty fever clutched me and I didn't rise from my bed for weeks. I prayed I would die, so they couldn't force me to be a witness against Sarah in the trial. I awakened howling from nightmares of my sister swinging from the gallows, her neck snapping in the noose.

But before they could pack Sarah off to York, she disappeared like a crow winging away into the clear blue of a summer's morning. She slipped from her cell as if by magic, though it's more likely one of the prison master's apprentices took pity and helped her escape. Though the bailiffs and the constable's men scoured Whitby and the surrounding moors, my sister was never seen again.

In our village, they've made her into a legend. The women washing at the beck sing ballads of our Sarah, and the men who drink at The Silent Woman spin tales. They say she escaped to live in some wild sea cave like a true sea witch, taking her revenge by luring ships to crash against the cliffs. Whenever the news of a gale or shipwreck comes round, they say it was Sarah's handiwork. But my heart tells me that Sarah stowed away on some ship to seek her fortune in a faraway land.

As for me, I've grown into a bold spinster. After Father died, I took over his trade as a bonesetter. Since my sister's exodus, my neighbours have held me in awe, as if they suspect that I, too, could cause myself to vanish. With each passing year, I become more and more like

Sarah—wilful, contrary, and full of myself. Behind my back, they call me shrew and worse, but not witch. The days of witch hunts have ended, for now the judges and educated folk have declared there's no such thing as witchcraft.

Along with bonesetting, I practice midwifery, having apprenticed with a woman from the next village. So now I am well-versed in the forbidden knowledge of which herbs can hinder conception and which can loosen a babe from the womb. But I also know what remedies can mend a grieving heart and summon back a lost love. They come to me in secret, the maidens, the wives, the spinsters, and the widows.

Three is a magic number. My mother died in gaol. My sister had to flee. But I am the third one who will not be banished. There are mornings when I awaken to them calling me, Rebecca and Sarah. When I feel their tug on me, drawing me out of the cottage and into the wind and sunlight of the high moors. I let them guide me back to the hill where I watch the land tumble into the sea and the sea unfurl to touch the sky. I hear them singing my name until my face is wet and I taste the brine. I answer their call, and then we are One.

THE WIZARD'S PLACE
CHRIS SIMMS

'Someone's in there,' Thomas announced, wind dragging his fringe across his eyes as he glanced over the top of the binoculars. He pushed the fair strands aside and took another look.

'Wizard's Place? Never,' his companion replied, ending his examination of the scudding clouds above them by rolling onto his front. 'Where?'

'He was in the garden, talking on the phone. Gone inside now.'

'Let's have them.'

Thomas handed the binoculars across. Harsh caws carried on the fast-moving air. He angled his head. Five choughs, black wings expertly caressing the jagged currents. The birds swept above the rocky outcrop, hung for a second to check the two boys out, then swiftly tumbled down the other side.

'Can't see anything.'

'He went inside,' Thomas replied. White like a boat, the lone building seemed to be drifting in the sea of fields below them.

'Are you sure?'

'Yeah, a grown-up. Dark coat on. Talking away, he was.'

'A hiker maybe? Using the cottage to kip in?'

Thomas thought for a moment. 'He didn't look like a hiker. Coat was leather for a start. Trendy and black.'

Michael wrinkled his nose. 'No sign of a car or anything.'

Thomas suddenly pointed off to the side. 'There she is! Going across the gully.'

The sharp movement of grey wings stood out against the motionless heather carpet. Keeping low, the falcon followed a crease in the moor, vanishing as the land sloped towards the coast's sheer cliffs. 'She had something again. I reckon she lives over there.'

Michael was still sweeping the binoculars about. 'Let's see if she comes back.'

The sun slowly sank into a band of cloud on the horizon, and as the light began to fade, a cold edge crept into the breeze. From the way Michael was silently glued to the eyepieces, Thomas could tell his friend was frustrated. He'd missed the peregrine passing yet again and he'd missed the mysterious figure in The Wizard's Place. Thomas quietly waited.

The name of the abandoned farmhouse had evolved within their group. It was known in the village as The White Cottage. But, to the boys, its solitary position made it seem an ideal home for someone who wanted to keep away from other people. Someone like a wizard; a white wizard because of the bleached walls and roof. The White Wizard's Place soon contracted to just The Wizard's Place.

'I'm cold,' Michael eventually muttered.

'Me too,' Thomas replied.

Michael rose on to his elbows and sat back on his knees. 'Call it a day?'

'OK.' Thomas followed suit, brushing bits of lichen from his top as his friend returned the binoculars to their case. 'We could try tomorrow.'

'Yeah, OK. Meet at The Monument?' Michael replied, taking a last look at the black windows of the derelict building.

Thomas was on his feet. 'I wonder what he's up to.'

Less than fifty metres down the narrow trail leading from the top, Thomas suddenly stopped. 'Adder!'

Michael craned his neck to see round the other boy. 'Cool.'

They watched the reptile emerge from the purple heather, head lifted slightly as it tested the air. It altered direction, moving purposefully to a cleft in the loose rocks. Its body slipped inside like liquid draining away.

The man reached up to the piece of dark material covering the window. The drawing pin attaching it to the frame dug into his thumb as he pressed it fully in. Satisfied it would hold, he dropped his hand and stepped back. The room was gloomy and smelled of disuse. He guessed, at one time, it had served as the farmer's general living area. The only other room on the ground floor had a trough-like sink attached to the wall. So that would have been the kitchen. The back door was bricked-up and the stairs had collapsed long ago. The ceilings were going the same way. Still, the roof was in good nick: the place was dry, even if bloody cold.

He knelt down. Now all the windows were properly blacked-out, he turned the control of the lamp up. A cluster of LED bulbs glowed more brightly, shadows shrank back. On the floor next to him was an inflatable mattress and sleeping bag. A two-ring burner was mounted on a breezeblock, cartons of UHT milk and tins of food lined alongside. From the other side of the room came a faint groan. The man looked at the blindfolded boy chained to the iron ring set in the wall. 'Shut it.'

Next morning, Thomas and Michael were sitting on the steps of the war memorial in the centre of the tiny village. A little way along was where, during term-time, the bus picked them up and drove the eight miles along a narrow country lane to the nearest primary school in St Davids.

'Seen this?' Clive asked breathlessly, approaching from the direction of the post office, a copy of the local paper in his hand.

'What's up?' Michael asked.

'A robbery, that's what. The post office in St Davids. Mr Rees isn't looking happy, I can tell you.' He glanced back at the modest building that also served as a convenience store and newsagents. 'Probably thinking he's next.'

'Who robbed it?' Michael asked. 'Did they get caught?'

'He,' Clive corrected him. 'Did *he* get caught. No, he didn't. Walked in at ten to three and said there was a gun under his coat. He took all the cash and walked back out.' Clive spread the paper out on the top step. Its front page was dominated by a photo of the St Davids' post office with police officers outside it. 'They're looking for a man about six foot tall wearing a long black leather coat.'

Michael's and Thomas' eyes touched.

'There's a thousand pound reward,' Clive continued, now ponderously reading from the final paragraph, 'for information leading to his arrest.'

Michael spoke directly at Thomas. 'A thousand pound reward?'

Clive picked up on the other boy's tone. 'What?'

'Someone's hiding out at The Wizard's Place,' Michael said quietly. 'We were on the Fortress and Thomas saw him.'

Clive looked at Thomas. 'What was he doing there?'

'Talking on his phone in the front garden. Then he went inside.'

Clive's eyes went from boy to boy. He grinned. 'Good one, you had me going.'

'No joke,' Michael shot back. 'Tell him, Thomas. What was he wearing?'

'A black leather coat.'

'What about a black leather coat?' a loud voice demanded.

All three heads turned. It was Gethyn, leader of their group purely through his size and the force of his punch.

Michael quickly spoke up. 'There's a man out at The Wizard's Place. We think it's the guy who robbed the post office in St Davids. He was wearing the same coat.'

Gethyn put his hands on his hips. 'How do you know?'

'We were up on The Fortress. Spotted him from there.'

'It was black leather, this coat?'

Michael nodded eagerly.

'You said just now Thomas saw him, not you,' Clive accused.

Thomas hated this: as soon as Gethyn showed up, everyone started behaving differently, all trying to impress the larger boy.

'Well?' Gethyn demanded, looking down at Thomas.

Thomas flicked a glance at Michael, caught the pleading look in his eyes. 'We both glimpsed him, but I had the binoculars. It was definitely a black leather coat he had on.'

Gethyn sat down on the edge of a step. He tapped his fingers rapidly against his knees for a few moments. 'Right, first thing, don't say a word about this to anyone. If it's just us, that's more reward money each, yeah?'

Michael and Clive obediently nodded.

Gethyn's head swivelled to Thomas. 'Yeah?'

Thomas had only moved to the village the previous year, and since then he'd struggled to be accepted by the other boys. And, without Gethyn's approval, he sensed he always would. 'OK,' he answered quietly.

'Information leading to his arrest,' Gethyn said, focus switching to Michael. 'Your dad has a proper camera, doesn't he? One with a zoom.'

'Yeah, for his work. He won't let me touch it though.'

Gethyn rolled his eyes. 'You don't ask him. Sneak it out, he won't know.'

'But if he – '

'But if he,' Gethyn echoed in a whine-filled voice. 'What are you, a girl? We meet back here at three. Michael, bring that camera.'

'Why three?' Thomas asked.

'Helping my Dad out,' Gethyn replied proudly, glance going to the butcher's shop alongside the post office.

The man bent over the little stove and sighed. Over five minutes to boil water for a brew. What a drag. He lay back on the inflatable mattress and slid the mobile from his coat pocket. The message in the top corner of the screen was the same: service unavailable. Morgan hadn't allowed for no phone signal in his brilliant plan, had he? Oh no, completely slipped his mind, that.

The man toyed with the idea of stepping outside. There was a single bar of reception if he stood about ten metres in front of the house. Would there be a message waiting? Even a text. Just something to say what the situation was.

But Morgan had forbidden him to leave the cottage during daylight hours. He sighed again and looked round. The window coverings meant he could hardly see. From the other side of the room came a whisper.

'What?' he said, knowing the answer already.

'Please Sir, the toilet.'

He caricatured the boy's Indian accent. 'Oh deary, deary me!' Chocolate wrappers and an empty bottle of Coke were next to his blankets. 'Drink less fizz and you won't need to piss.'

'Yes, sorry.' Blindfold round his head, the young lad was trying to get up, inner wrists pressed together by the plastic tie. The chain rattled as he fell weakly against the wall.

The man shook his head, thinking the bucket in the kitchen would need emptying soon. 'Wait,' he ordered, patting his coat pockets for the padlock key.

The rocks forming the rim of The Fortress faintly resembled castle battlements. The boys approached it by the cliff path that hugged the coast. Out of sight below them was a beach used as a nursery by grey seals.

The noise of the pups carried up to them. The young animals sounded like a food-poisoned class of infants, moaning in pain. Gethyn tore a clod of earth from the side of the path and lobbed it over the edge. 'Stop your stupid noise.'

Half an hour later, they approached The Fortress' summit on all fours. Inland stood The Wizard's Place. Gethyn clicked his fingers. 'Give us the binoculars.'

Thomas handed them across without a word. Beside him, Michael extracted his father's digital camera from its case with infinite care.

By dusk, they hadn't spotted any movement. Thomas saw the falcon pass at one point, but he kept quiet. Gethyn would probably only try and rob its nest, come the spring. The larger boy reached out to Michael and jabbed a knuckle into his ribs. 'You better not've been telling porkies.'

Michael shrank back. 'No, he was there.'

Thomas could see Gethyn's fingers forming into a fist, ready to deliver a dead arm to the cowering Michael. 'Hey, Gethyn, we saw an adder yesterday. Looking for a hibernation spot, I reckon.'

Gethyn's hand dropped. 'Really?'

The man peeled the corner of window covering back. The light had faded outside. The lad in the corner was sleeping fitfully, whimpering every now and again. The noise was becoming really annoying. Climbing out of his sleeping bag, the man circled his arms about and then put on his coat. The evening air was cold, but it was a relief to be out of the dingy building. He moved forward a few steps, eyes on the screen of the mobile phone held out before him.

It was the blue glow that caught Thomas' eye. 'There he is.'

The other three boys scrabbled to the edge. Gethyn had positioned the binoculars earlier and only needed to look through the eye pieces. 'It's a man! Michael, get his picture, quick!'

Michael began fumbling with the camera's zoom.

The man stared at the lit screen. One bar flickered briefly to two. He waited for a phone message alert to ping up. 'Come on, come on,' he said under his breath. Nothing. So typical of bloody Morgan, he thought bitterly. It had always been like this: Morgan coming up with his schemes and giving out orders. And who, the man thought, gets the shit end of the stick? Me. He looked back at the cottage. Its white-washed walls seemed to shine in the half-light. Shuddering at the thought of its cold rooms, the man wondered whether to just call and find out what the hell was going on. But that would go against Morgan's strict orders. No using the phone except in an emergency. The man slid it into his pocket and trudged back towards the house.

'Let's see, let's see!' Gethyn hissed.

They were huddled round the camera's screen, a few metres back from the summit. Michael scrolled through the images. The figure was just a faint shadow in the distant garden. Michael tried zooming in, but the shot turned grainy and lost all definition.

The bell above the post office door gave a ding as the four boys trooped in. Mr Rees looked up nervously from behind the counter. He gave a strained smile. 'Good morning boys, you look like you're on a mission. Sweets, is it?'

Gethyn was in front. 'We were wondering, Mr Rees, is there anything else about that robbery in St Davids?'

Copies of the day's local paper were stacked on the counter. The front page story had now reverted to the kidnap of a wealthy Indian businessman's son, snatched a few days before from the grounds of his father's country retreat. 'Nope, police are still looking.'

Gethyn pretended to think. 'Oh, you know it said about a reward for information. What does that mean? Would a photo be enough, you reckon?'

'A photo?' The elderly man's eyes went to the CCTV camera near the ceiling. 'If it's of his face, yes. So they can make a match with footage from the post office in St Davids. I just hope they get him sharpish.'

'Right, thanks Mr Rees,' Gethyn replied as they all started backing away. But the post office manager's fingers were now brushing at his upper lip and he didn't seem to hear.

'How do we get his face?' Clive said glumly as they ambled across to the war memorial. 'He never comes out until its dark.'

'I know,' Gethyn replied, lips twitching with the start of a smile. He looked at Thomas. 'Where did you see that adder, again?'

'Wake up.' The man looked down at the boy's huddled form. He knew teenagers could sleep for hours, but the kid wasn't even ten. 'Wake up!'

The boy's head shifted a bit.

The man pulled his blankets back. He was on his side in the foetal position. The man recalled the moaning and groaning that had gone on during the night. He'd assumed the youngster was having nightmares. Now he wasn't so sure.

'Can you hear me?' he asked, bending down.

The boy's breathing was fluttery and fast.

'Jesus Christ,' the man cursed, removing the balaclava from his coat pocket and rolling it over his head. Once his face was concealed, he yanked the lad's blindfold off. His eyes were slightly open, but in an unfocused sort of way. The man held a hand out and clicked his fingers. The boy blinked, once. Crouching down, the man held a palm against the boy's forehead. Hot. Way too hot.

The man had an inkling of what the problem was. He looked at the boy's hands, tucked in between his knees. Carefully, he pulled at the boy's wrist. The youngster put up some feeble resistance, but the man easily forced the boy's hands up. He examined the bandaging wrapped around the boy's left fingers. No new blood was showing beneath it, but the skin around the stump of his third finger was red and shiny.

The man recalled the time when, as a child, he'd got appendicitis. The doctors had pressed their fingers into his lower stomach and suddenly let go. It was some kind of test for whether infection had set in. The man gently squeezed what remained of the boy's finger and then released it. A howl filled the room.

The boys walked in single file along the trail leading down from the top of The Fortress. Gethyn led the way, an empty plastic fertiliser sack in one hand. It swayed with the adder's weight. Once they'd lifted back the big stone, getting the snake had been easy. Curled in a corner, drowsy with the urge to hibernate, it couldn't react fast enough to the forked stick's descent.

The man stared at his phone. Morgan would go ballistic if he called, but Morgan wasn't stuck in an unheated cottage with a delirious youngster. His mind went back through the years. While Morgan and his mates did the nicking, it was his job to distract the shopkeeper with some sob-story about losing his mum. Fine when the shop keeper didn't spot the other boys jamming stuff into their pockets. Not so good when he did, and grabbed their little accomplice by the neck as the others bolted out the door.

The man checked out the window. No one was around. No one was ever around; the place was in the middle of nowhere. He stepped outside and made the call.

'This better be good, ringing me at this time.'

'We've got a problem,' the man answered, scuffing at the loose stones by his feet.

'Oh yeah?'

'The merchandise? It's... it's going bad. An infection, I reckon.'

'Payment is almost made. The sample we sent helped.'

Sample, the man thought. That's what's caused this problem. And Morgan snipping off the boy's finger was never part of the plan. 'The state of the merchandise is really worrying me.'

'I just said, payment is due. Once it's been made, a car will come by.'

'And... and the merchandise?'

'Next morning, its location will be given.'

The man glanced back at the cottage. 'The state of the merchandise is not good. It might have gone off by then. Totally off, I mean.'

Morgan's voice hardened. 'That's the score. Don't ring again.'

The boys crept along the overgrown lane which led up to The Wizard's Place, stopping when the tip of a white chimney came into view.

'Right, here's how we'll do it,' Gethyn whispered, grip tight on the neck of the sack. 'Michael, you get the camera all set up. Zoomed in on the front porch. When he comes out, he'll be crapping his pants. He won't notice us. A few quick snaps and we're off. Got it?'

The other three boys exchanged confused glances.

'He'll be crapping his pants, why?' Clive asked.

'The adder, stupid,' Gethyn replied. 'No way he'll stay inside with it in there.'

'But,' Michael murmured, 'how will the snake get inside the cottage?'

Gethyn turned to Thomas. 'That's where you come in.'

Thomas looked up at the larger boy. 'Me?'

'You want to be mates with us?' Gethyn asked. 'Then you'll do this.'

Thomas turned to the other two. A smile of relief was on Clive's face. Michael had looked away.

The man regarded the boy in silence. A shallow pant now filled the room. The swelling had extended across his knuckles and down the back of his hand. He didn't seem to hear anything. Always, the man thought, me. The crap deal, the worst job. Well, bollocks to this.

The rough drive had a strip of grass growing in its middle. Patches of clover dotted it. A cricket whirred in the undergrowth to his side.

Thomas slowly edged forward, holding the fertiliser sack as far from him as he could. As he neared the crudely built porch, the front door came into view. At its centre was the large letter box. He moved off to the right, hoping to see in the nearest window. There was grey netting in its lower half. Behind it, the blackness seemed unnatural. Too uniform. Was it dark material hanging there? Yes, but rumpled in one corner. He put his face to the dirty glass and peeped through the triangular gap. A lamp was on. Beside it, a cooking stove, tins. Something was on the other side of the room, attached to the wall by a chain.

The man paused behind the front door and took out his phone. He pressed the green button. The screen started to flicker its way through the start-up sequence.

Face pressed to the window, Thomas could make out a head. A boy's head! He was lying on the – A creak to his left. The man was right there, a phone in his hand. The shock of his appearance caused Thomas to step back and his balance was lost. As he fell, his arms went up.

The sack opened above him and he saw a tight grouping of black diamonds rapidly stretching out, hard cold eyes coming straight at his. The pinkness inside its gaping mouth. He twisted his head and the pain in his throat was like a hundred wasp stings all at once. As he lay gasping on his back, he heard the thud of footsteps as the others ran away.

The man tried to take it all in: a slender, blonde-haired kid lying on his back, a snake moving fast across the dry ground. Other kids pegging it down the rough drive. It was an adder. A big one, too. The boy's eyes were wide with pain and his fingertips were dug into the ground. A rustle as the snake vanished into dry undergrowth.

Cautiously, the man stepped closer to the boy. He could see a red spot on the lad's neck, skin rising around it like bread dough. He looked off down the driveway. A camera was lying there, bits of black plastic broken off where it had hit the ground.

'They put you up to this?'

The boy didn't reply. Couldn't. The man judged times and distances. Two or three miles back to the nearest village. The other boys wouldn't be raising the alarm for a bit. Time enough to pack his stuff, call Morgan and arrange for the car to collect him from somewhere nearby.

From the wheeze in the boy's breathing and the way his lips were puffing out, the man could tell the lad's airway was closing up. He looked down the driveway and saw, in the space where the other boys had been, his own life.

The crew from the air ambulance had been in the cottage less than ten minutes before he heard sirens approaching. He continued to watch the medics as they went about their work. Both boys were now attached to makeshift drips and the medics' voices were a lot more relaxed. Vehicles started pulling up outside, so he stepped from the cottage into bright daylight.

The first police officers were half out of their car. One saw him and pointed a finger. 'You the one who called this in?'

The man nodded, arms at his sides.

The officer was reaching for the cuffs on his utility belt. 'You're Ian Todd?'

The man nodded again. 'And I've got some other names for you.'

THE MAN WHO DIDN'T BREATHE

JIM KELLY

Jed had read that every living thing has the same number of heartbeats in its life. So the faster you live the quicker you die.

Life slowed down for Jed the day one of the fishermen in the cove told him that a common seal, in winter, could reduce its heart rate to just four beats a minute when diving in icy water. Out on his surfboard, in his winter suit, he'd see them sometimes, the common and the grey, ghosting by beneath him. The common had V-shaped nostrils, glistening and black like a dog's. Once, a white adult male, scarred along its back like some warrior Leviathan, had hung beneath him in the current absolutely stationary, and released a single bubble of air, which rose up not as a perfect sphere, but as a strange, buckling, envelope, a gyroscopic diamond rushing towards the light, to pop inaudibly at the surface.

Jed, sixteen, thought a lot more about holding his breath, about slowing the heart that was propelling him, headlong, towards his own death. On Google he found that a Norwegian called Stig Severinsen had the world record for holding your breath under water at twenty-two minutes. Jed kicked the tyres on that one, and found that in so-called 'static apnea' you were allowed to pump your blood full of pure oxygen before you dropped beneath the water. So that didn't count. But the *unassisted* world record was still eleven minutes thirty-five seconds.

There were tricks of the trade too: like 'lung packing' – drawing parcels of air down your open gullet, keeping your epiglottis tucked away, or hyperventilating to charge the blood up with oxygen, or meditation, to slow the metabolism. The first time Jed tried it, really went for it, was during his second year on Freshwater West, on the lifeguard gig. He could see his mum's house from out at sea, a pale whitewashed cottage on the cliffs. If the sea was up she'd sit outside and watch him surf. But that day he'd been out on the board for an hour and he hadn't seen the ocean crease, let alone break, and so he'd just slipped into the water and hung there, face down, willing his heart to slow, as if it pumped honey, not air. His mum had reluctantly given him a diver's watch for Christmas, so he accurately clocked that first attempt at eighty-three seconds. Buying a new notebook, a different colour from the rest, he recorded the date and the time achieved.

Beneath the water he felt free. Awkward, shy, distant, he'd always felt like an outsider in the real world. Now, if he trained, he could inhabit another world. When he woke up each morning during that winter the first thing he saw was the image of his own body, in its wet-suit, hanging in the water. Sometimes he wondered if that was where he went when he was asleep, if he regressed in time to the distant Jurassic age when what became man had emerged from the sea, dragging itself up the beach on bony fins. He drew strength from this idea of himself as an almost prehistoric life force.

By the August Bank Holiday of his third year he could stay down for a few seconds short of four minutes. There was a spot, a hundred yards north-west off the third beach groyne, where a subterranean sand bank rose to within ten foot of the surface. This shallow, tear-shaped, stretch of sea glowed a turquoise green under the sun, the light reflected up from the white quartz below. The beach crowd which hung round the lifeguard hut laughed when he did his meditation on the edge of the dunes, sat like a Buddha, palms up to the sun; but that day, when he said he'd break four minutes, they'd all swum out and formed a circle, as he took a super breath and dropped to the white sand below, to lay, like a star fish, watching feet tread water above his head.

The air trickled out of him, and he felt his buoyancy seep away, so that the water seemed to press him down into the sand. Waiting until the second hand passed the four minute mark he kicked away, and floating up he felt the roar of victory in his throat. Exploding out in a splash he heard them clapping, cheering, and that was when he first saw Amber: an identikit beach girl, with blonde hair and a biscuit tan, in a bikini not a wetsuit, watching his eyes, because he watched hers: they weren't amber – he'd looked the colour up on Wiki later, but they weren't brown either, they had a kind of yellow fleck of light close to the centre, which if he hadn't been starved of oxygen in that first moment he might have noticed made her look malevolent: a cat's eye.

A month later, lying on the rattan mats by the lifeguards' hut, she let him put suntan lotion on her back, allowing his fingers to run down her spine, into the gentle dip. Then, adding a fresh dollop of the white cream to his palm, he ran his hand along her arm, feeling the heat it generated, the sticky down on her skin. Eyes on the sea, he traced the smooth sinuous line of her hand and then, with a little visceral shock, the cold surface of an unknown object, metallic and cold.

'Who gave you that ?' he said, and only later thought he'd made a mistake, the way he'd let an immediate sense of entitlement shine through, giving credence to the idea that he had a right, an authority, over her body.

The ring was silver, quite broad for a woman's, and very bright, polished by the gritty, hard, particles of beach sand. The stone was yellow, about the size of the fingernail on her little finger. She turned on to her back, pulling a towel deftly across her breasts, and held it out for him to see – not just out, *but up,* so that the light shone through it and he could see it wasn't clear at all, but like molasses, shot through with little bubbles of rising air, and in the middle an insect set – fossilized – caught forever at the moment the precious stone was created.

'It's amber,' she said, as if that was an answer to his question. 'My special subject.' She smiled, and he felt a fool, and the sun went cold. 'So there's grey amber – that's ambergris, and it comes out of sperm whales. Like, literally...' She mimicked a vomit. 'It's used for incense, and perfume, and to ward off death. It washes ashore, but it's like super-rare. And there's yellow amber, like this, which is a tree resin, and I guess it's just beautiful, and it washes ashore too; well, sometimes. I guess the sea breaks it out of the rocks in the cliffs and stuff.'

She still hadn't answered his question: 'I should have told you,' she said at last, and he knew then he'd just walked right into this moment, as if it was a trap, and he was stuck, like the prehistoric insect in the precious stone.

She made telling him the truth sound like a favour. The ring was a present from Eddie, her boyfriend, who lived in Bristol and ran a music shop, selling vinyl, and posters, and stuff like that. Eddie was twenty, she added, as if it was some kind of first class degree. She'd come up to Freshwater with her friends to stay with her aunt in the village but now Eddie was due – like some kind of comet. He'd drive down, in his van. They'd sleep in the van. It had been great, she said, getting to know Jed. She'd had a good time. She was sorry, she said again, that she hadn't said something sooner.

Taking the ring off she let him hold it, as if he was a child, to be bought off with a trinket. The captured insect, with its black carapace and bowed legs, looked alien. Jed thought he could hear the electric buzz of its wings, held tight inside the ancient resin, and in that moment the ring fell but Amber caught it with a smooth, effortless, grace. For a moment the wide beach-girl smile slipped and Jed thought he saw anger, and the yellow light of pity.

He stood: 'It's been fun,' he said in what sounded like someone else's voice, and then he ran towards the sea, showing her his heels. Swimming out, breaststroke, he went beyond the outer breakers, where the surfers waited in a school to catch a wave. Tumbling, he nose-dived, until the water turned from green to blue, then edged to a strange spectral violet – shot through with slivers of light from above. The ocean floor emerged – ribbed, like an old man, a lobster scuttling, a conger eel cruising. His eardrums pinked with the pressure.

Settling, he knelt on the cold sand and folded himself into a ball and wondered, if he did cry, what would happen to the tears. Four minutes went past. He didn't have his diver's watch, but by the time he opened his eyes and looked to the surface it was almost too late: his heart beat was a distant, weak, footfall, and a slow blunt pain was crossing his brain like an eclipse. Dying at that moment, as airless as a rock, would have been a strange achievement.

Instead, energized by an emotion he didn't recognize, he unfurled himself from the foetal ball, and forced his body into an aerodynamic arrow, rising up. As he twisted away from the ocean floor he caught sight, for the first time, on the very edge of vision, the outline of a wreck. The steel hull of a coaster, with a broken back, lay in the silt, a communications mast at an angle, the white sand over its starboard side, like a shroud. Ships' ropes and twisted cables drifted with the current. The image lived for a second, but he knew he'd have it with him always.

When he finally broke the surface he opened his mouth and the air rushed in, inflating his lungs, and he lay there, on his back, gasping, watching a white cloud the size of a housing estate glide past. Amber came into his mind, and Eddie's van, and while he never really had a plan – in the sense of an ordered series of cause and effect – he always knew, from that moment, how it would end.

When Eddie arrived it was immediately apparent he was no surfer. Short, muscled, with jet black curls, and swirls of more hair on his chest and back, he had a kind of blunt power, but not a trace of the necessary balance, grace or agility. Early morning, when Jed came down to take his watch, the windows of Eddie's van were clouded with a blush of condensation. Eddie joined in the beach volleyball, and the BBQs by the lifeguard hut, but when he swam Jed noted that he always stayed shore-side of the big breakers, and that there was something frantic about his breathing when he came up from a whiteout; as if he was having a panic attack.

Jed waited. It was his job to chalk up the wind speed, the swell, and the sea temperature on an A-board by the wooden steps to the car park. That day, the last Monday of the season, the wave height was seven foot six, with a good westerly swell rolling in off the Atlantic, the last echoes of a Caribbean hurricane called Justine. The sea temperature was just 13C – chilly, a harbinger of winter, but just right, because it meant that winter wet suits were back. His own was a tight fit from last year, but would do, and he found another from the store at the water sports hut which he slung over his shoulder: a Seasprite '15, with a flash lightning bolt design. Lee, the head lifeguard, gave him a spare board, which was waxed up, and had a new tether. Strolling north along the beach he searched for their windbreak. Amber, topless, lay on her front. Eddie was smoking, listening to an iPod, his eyes on the white water.

'Hi,' said Jed, and Amber twisted her head round to smile.

Eddie gave him a strange look.

'I'm off shift,' said Jed. 'I thought Eddie might like to check out the water. The crew's down towards the harbour – but it's flatter here, better for a debut performance...'

Eddie, one earpiece out, was very still.

'I've got winter suits. Could be the last good day for weeks. And the sun's a real bonus. You gotta do it!'

Jed pointed out to sea, at the churning colour, the ozone-heavy onshore breeze, the full Atlantic rumble of the waves dumping sand and rock.

'There's a storm coming,' he added. 'Jagged water right, that's no good. You need the swell. A good clean swell that's come all the way from America.'

Jed had judged the patronizing tone perfectly.

'I know,' said Eddie, his Adam's Apple bobbing.

'Go on,' said Amber, turning over, not bothering this time with the towel: 'You said you would. You promised.' The last word she lisped, like it was a private joke.

'A low centre of gravity's good...' offered Jed.

Eddie put the suit on really quickly, as if his courage might fail. Then they punted the boards into the shallows and breasted the first set of six breakers. Jed leading the way, powered out, beyond the white fizzing lines which ran parallel to the beach, the ghosts of broken waves.

Eddie, both arms over his board as if it was a life raft, couldn't take his eyes off the open sea, as if a killer wave was out there, brewing.

'We're too far out, kid' he shouted, and Jed just put a thumb up, and pointed a mile out, where a jagged line was boiling.

Jed had several scenarios in his head, all of which relied on getting

Eddie exhausted, for, while he might be a klutz on a board, he had enough power in his stocky thighs to kick out and break a bone.

But in the end the sea was Jed's accomplice.

The wave that wiped Eddie out was a one-off; awesome, rearing up, twelve feet of glassy blue water, it fell on him with a tectonic shudder, driving his body down, squeezing the air out of his lungs. When he came up, dazed, there was blood on his forehead where the skeg had caught him, the board bouncing back on its elastic tether. His eyes seemed to search the water for something solid – anything, a buoy, some seaweed, a piece of flotsam, but the whole of the world was water and sky. His mouth seemed to be seeping white water, as he threw an arm over the surfboard, without the strength to haul himself on top.

Jed took a chance and rode a swell, low in the water, his own board floating free, quickly surveying the distant beach. Amber was just visible, still out flat in the sand. The rest of Freshwater West was deserted, but for a crowd by the lifeguard hut and the beach café.

Slipping his ankle tether he reeled in his board and then shot it seawards, skimming it thirty feet, so that it bobbed beyond the wave-line. Diving down he hung beneath the churning swell. The power of the waves fell away geometrically with water depth, so that just a few feet beneath the white, fizzing, spume the sea was still, a glassy semi-solid. Eddie's legs hung in the water like dead weights, encapsulated in the black suit, twenty feet away. Jed swam over and eased apart the Velcro ankle strap which held the line to his board.

Surfacing he filled his lungs one last time, then slid down until he could grip Eddie's left ankle. Sinking further he gave the body a violent, downward, jolt.

Eddie came alive then, the last air billowing from his lungs, his arms thrashing for the surface – that precious borderland with the air, which glistened a few feet above his head, a sheet of mercury silver. For a minute, or less, Jed kept the downward pressure on Eddie's leg, willing his own heart to slow its rapid beat. The danger was a real one, that he'd expend too much oxygen in the fight, and then fail to make the descent. But Eddie's arm movements became quickly sporadic, then slowed, then stopped. There was one last spasm, and then he hung lifeless, and Jed slipped his hand through the ankle strap, and began to tow him down.

Out of the gloom the top of the communications mast on the coaster was the first thing to appear, as if it was rising up of its own accord. He'd dived many times to explore the wreck since that first sighting, and had found the name: MARIA ASSUMPTA on the prow, and a code for the homeport of ESBIO. Checking in the pilot's book at the dock office he'd found this meant it was registered in Bilbao, Spain. He'd thought about finding out all the details: when she'd sank, if anyone had died, her cargo, but then he'd stopped himself because he didn't want to leave a trail, even on his laptop. Once, he'd got into the small bridge through one of the shattered portholes, and there'd been something on the floor, wrapped round the base of the helmsman's chair, but his nerve had gone, and in a fizz of air bubbles he'd bolted, rising up, his heart beat out of control.

There were no air bubbles from Eddie.

After a fine summer, with still water, the visibility was good, the sunlight filtering down, so that the MARIA ASSUMPTA threw a shadow on the ocean floor. The wreck lay about him, in its skin of silt and rust, which seemed to blur the edges of the steel, and combined with the buckling effect of the current to make the scene dreamlike, as if it all pulsed in time with Jed's slow, thudding heart.

Time was running out. The rope from the forward winch, floating vertically free, was split about thirty feet along its length, the rough fibres divided around an eye-shaped hole, into which he thrust Eddie's foot, still encased in the wetsuit boot. It was a tight fit, and he struggled to get the whole of the boot tread through the narrow gap. But, finally, the foot was snared: bait on a hook, he thought, pleased with the image.

The light here, at a depth of around eight fathoms, seemed to not only fall from above but radiate from within the water, as if the broken ship, and the floating body, and the idling incurious fish, were phosphorescent. Eddie's eyes shone too, wide open now, with blood vessels broken in the whites. One of the wet suit mittens had come free of the right hand and so Jed gently pulled it back on, a finger at a time, until it was snug.

Floating upwards and away the last thing Jed saw was Eddie's jet black hair, whorled on his skull in a double crown, the locks pulsing like a coral. Fading to grey, he lost sight of him completely, well before he surfaced.

They found Eddie's board within an hour, along towards the creek, and the skeg still held a smear of skin, blood and hair from the wound on the head. Jed found that the tears came easily. The story he kept simple, never embellishing the details, so that the lifeguards, and then the police, had never suspected it was anything more than the truth. He'd seen the wave that had wiped Eddie out, but he'd dived beneath it. Eddie had said he'd surfed before, that he was no novice, but Jed blamed himself for taking him out in the swell. Amber, distraught as she listened that first time, had broken free and got in the water, collapsing in the shallows, running her hands through the sand – half liquid, half solid. When they'd got her out and on a stretcher by the hut Jed had felt a surge of... what ? He found it difficult to categorize his emotions. The closest he could get was that it felt like a taste of glory, because the amber ring was gone, plucked off by the sand.

The search for Eddie's body was what journalists like to call a running story. The Pembrokeshire currents were notorious, and so they looked on the beaches near Wexford, and even on the Breton coast. Helpfully, a trawler captain reported a sighting of what might have been a body in the water nearly two hundred miles south-west of Freshwater. Then, the next day, a passenger on the Stranraer to Larne ferry said she'd seen a body in a wet suit when she'd been looking for whales, although Jed felt this 'sighting' was judged unreliable. But it all helped create a sense of inevitable oblivion. Eddie was gone. The sea had taken him forever.

It should have been the end. It *felt* like the end, a month later, in an icy late-October sea, when he swam out and dived down towards the wreck of the Maria Assumpta. The full winter wet suit held Eddie's rotting body within its rubber envelope. The head, already picked clean of flesh, was skull-white, although Jed didn't linger to note the details. His point-of-view, his perspective, was very different. In the minute he had left he swam north, so that he could turn and see the scene back-lit, as it were, by the low autumnal sunlight filtering down from above. An hour before the sunset, the light was blushed yellow and red, and Eddie's body hung like an insect, caught forever in its amber trap.

But it wasn't the end. Jed came ashore a week later to find Amber on the waterline, a hand round each elbow, shivering. She'd thanked him then, for the letter he'd written, and for being kind. Her face was not the same, it seemed to pulse with life – the skin flushed, the hair catching the light, as if he could see each individual strand. She was close enough to touch, and he'd felt his hand reaching out, but she was looking in her beach bag, and she produced a photograph and held it out, with a shy smile.

'Things have happened,' she said. 'I've come back. I'm going to live here, with my aunt. I'm really glad you're here, Jed.' She looked around: 'What do you do in the winter ?'

Jed shrugged: 'Wear a winter suit. ' They both laughed.

The picture wasn't what he'd expected at all. It was a hospital scan, an ultrasound image, of a foetus swimming in its amniotic fluid in the womb, tethered by the umbilical cord. Jed imagined tiny fish swimming past it, caught in a miniature visceral current.

'It's like it's been set in a jewel,' said Jed.

'It's Eddie's,' she said. 'It's a boy.'

THE STARLINGS
ANN CLEEVES

The letter arrived on her desk unopened. It had PERSONAL AND CONFIDENTIAL written in capitals at the top of the envelope. A square envelope, pale blue, so she thought before realizing how light it was, that it might contain a card. It happened to be her birthday. She set it aside because she was about to go into a meeting. An earnest young man from the Northumberland Wildlife Trust was making a formal complaint about the poisoning of hen harriers on a grouse moor in the centre of the county. Immediately afterwards there was an interview with a youth worker who'd been accused of grooming underage girls for sex. A normal day at Kimmerston Police Station but the encounters had left Inspector Vera Stanhope bruised and depressed. She didn't open the letter until she was about to leave for home.

Inside was a sheet of unlined paper covered with shaky handwriting. The signature at the bottom meant nothing to her but the first sentence brought back memories that were as painful and sharp as sleet on the face in a north easterly wind.

I was an acquaintance of your father's; we were for a while comrades in arms. It was the phrase comrades in arms that took her back nearly forty years.

Vera had been a teenager. Just a teenager. Awkward and lumpy, a loner, as embarrassed by the pity of sympathetic teachers as by the snide comments of the other kids. Her mother had died when she was small and Hector was no kind of father, but still it was the response of other people that had caused most pain. The girls' superior giggles at her confusion when she had her first period: 'Really, Vera. Don't you know anything?' The notes home offering help with second-hand uniform. The memories still made her blush with shame and fury.

Hector had been most involved in illegal egg-collection during those years. A distraction perhaps or a consolation for the death of his wife but Vera had been too young and too angry to see it that way. She'd been dragged along to keep watch as he plundered nests. An unwilling accomplice, but desperate to please. She pictured him still, a big man in boots and waterproofs, a rucksack on his back. From a distance he'd look like any other walker or climber but in his bag would be an egg box, cotton wool. The tools of his trade.

Collecting rare birds' eggs had been his passion and addiction. His enemies had been RSPB wardens and the police. He'd sit in his house at night, drinking cheap Scotch and rage about them. She'd decided even then that one day she'd join the police – it would be the ultimate rebellion. She'd do something about Hector and his shady contacts, the men he called his *comrades in arms*. One of whom had written the letter she held in her hand now.

Not that there'd been anything superficially shady about Edward Forbes. He was quiet, middle-aged, a bachelor. Thin hair. Red face. Hector had blustered and bullied him and Vera had felt a little sorry for him. Now she tried to remember how Forbes had earned a living. He'd had the air of an academic, but it came to her that he'd been book-keeper for a firm of solicitors. He'd lived in a cottage at the end of a track in the flat plain of south east Northumberland and driven every day to an office in the city. It had been strange schizophrenic existence, she thought now. One that mirrored her own life. She commuted from the house in the hills that had once been Hector's to the police station in Kimmerston. Forbes had aspired to be a country gentleman but had never quite made it.

Forbes had only stood up to Hector once and that had marked the end of their relationship. They might have been comrades in arms before the altercation but after the quarrel the men had never spoken again. So this invitation coming out of the blue after more than thirty years was disturbing. Vera couldn't imagine why an elderly man – he must be at least seventy – should want to see her. She worried that he might have something to confess. Something that might implicate Hector.

The letter was very precise. *If you feel you can spare the time please come to Grindon Cottage at 3.oopm on Sunday afternoon.* No suggestion that this might be inconvenient or that they might arrange a time and place to suit Vera. The only hint as to the reason for the summons: *I'm worried that it's happening again.* She was tempted to throw the letter into the bin, to pretend it had never arrived. She still felt unclean after the interview with the youth worker, a quiet tidy man who repeated his excuses as if she were foolish not to appreciate his reasoning: *'You must see that I understand these girls better even than their parents. I give them an education, support. They adore me. You do know, Inspector, that they'll never give evidence against me.'* When he was returned to the cell all she wanted was to be home, a large drink and a bath.

But curiosity got the better of her and on Sunday afternoon she drove up the track towards the house. It was November, grey and misty and evening had come early. A flock of starlings scattered ahead of her.

The place was smarter. Perhaps Forbes had achieved his ambition of respectability in retirement. The house had been freshly white-washed and there was a new conservatory facing towards the coast. There was a light inside, which shone through the hexagonal glass panes. Vera glanced in before knocking at the door. The curiosity again. Edward Forbes didn't look very different. He'd always seemed old to Vera. He sat in a cane rocking chair which had a sheepskin thrown over the back. His hair was still thin. And he'd been shot in the chest. On the floor by the side of the chair lay an elderly shotgun. They would trace it to the dead man. But Vera already suspected that this was no suicide.

She stood in the gloom and tried to analyse her reaction. Why was she convinced that the man hadn't killed himself? A coroner might think that she'd been summoned to the house just for the purpose of finding the man's body and the letter could be seen as a suicide note. But perhaps this was what she'd expected from the moment she'd opened the envelope. An explosion of violence. Because Forbes had provoked anger in Hector and he'd suggested in the note that history was repeating itself. It came to her that she was glad Hector was dead because she might otherwise have suspected him of killing his former friend.

All the time she was on the phone to her colleagues, summoning the pathologist, arranging for the CSIs, discussing the case with Joe Ashworth, her mind was elsewhere. She was remembering her last meeting with Forbes and the row that had fractured his relationship with her father for ever. She tried to recreate the last time she'd seen the deceased man. It had been this time of year and this time of day. The starlings had been here then too, but a bigger flock, swirling and wheeling above her, before settling like soot on the bare trees.

The sound of a distant siren broke into her day dreams. It would be local officers, excited by the idea of a suspicious death on their patch. She climbed into the Land Rover that had once been Hector's and waited, and in her mind she was fourteen, unloved and ugly.

The last time she was here her father had sent her outside as if she was a child young enough to play. Or a dog. 'Edward and I need to talk.' She'd sat here, staring out at the ploughed field and the birds, but despite the cold the window had been open and she'd been curious even then so she'd heard what had been said.

The discussion was about someone who had died. So that too was history repeating itself. And that was all she could remember. She forced herself to concentrate, but it was so long ago that she was only left with the mood that she'd felt at the time – gloomy, bewildering, humiliating. A mood that even then had seemed to sum up her whole adolescence. Hector and Forbes had fought with words. There'd been no physical violence, not even any raised voices, but she'd been aware of a profound disagreement. The end of a friendship. She closed her eyes and thought that even an odd snatch of conversation might help.

When she opened them there was a face staring in through the Land Rover window. She was startled. At first she thought it might be the local officers, though the siren had been a long way off and even deep in thought surely she would have heard their car on the track. And the face belonged to an elderly woman. It had never occurred to Vera that someone else might have been in the cottage. She'd always pictured Forbes as a confirmed bachelor. The woman was pale and dishevelled with white hair straggling over her face. Vera felt ridiculous. She might be haunted by the past but Forbes' death could be something more commonplace – a domestic situation that had developed into a tragedy; she could see that this woman might have mental health problems. Vera opened the door of the Land Rover and the woman moved out of the way so she could climb out.

'Who are you?' The woman's voice was imperious.

Vera introduced herself.

'You'll have seen that Edward's shot himself. The bloody fool.'

'I can see that he's dead. No idea yet how it happened.'

The woman blinked as if she'd been slapped, but she showed no sign of distress.

'Who are you?' Vera thought the face was slightly familiar and wondered if perhaps the woman had been part of Hector's social scene all those years ago. There *had* been women in the group. Hangers-on. Wives. They'd made coffee and brought out sandwiches when business had been completed.

'I'm Margaret Lawlor.' As if the fact should be obvious.

Vera knew then who she was dealing with. The woman's family had once been almost royalty in this part of the country. They'd owned most of the land between the hills and the coast before Margaret's husband had gambled chunks of it away. 'You knew Edward Forbes?'

'Of course.' No explanation though Vera thought the man must have moved up the social ladder if he had the honourable Margaret as a chum.

'I'll need to talk to you later.' Vera could hear vehicles on the track now and the last thing she needed was this woman in the way.

'I'll be in.' Margaret shot Vera a glance. 'You'll know where to find me.' She walked away. She wore black wellingtons that flapped around thin legs and a long black PVC mackintosh. A crow fading into the dusk.

Vera left Joe Ashworth in charge of the crime scene and drove to the Lawlor place. As Forbes' cottage had become smarter, this house was obviously crumbling into disrepair. It was quite dark now, but in the Land Rover's headlights she could see the sagging gutters and the overgrown garden. It was a big Victorian pile. Margaret's family had owned mines and shipyards and had bought into the feudal lifestyle at the end of the nineteenth century. They hadn't inherited their wealth. As she walked over the gravel pierced with weeds Vera had a flash of memory: Forbes and Hector talking about their passion for egg-collecting at that last meeting. But then she distrusted her memory because the conversation had the same tone, the same self-justification and arrogance as that of the youth worker talking about his paedophilia.

'If we don't study these things and collect them' Forbes had said, *'the knowledge will be lost. We understand patterns of breeding birds better than the academics. This is the real science.'* Perhaps she was imagining the words. In any event at this point the men had still been in agreement. The argument had come later.

Margaret Lawlor opened the door to Vera. She'd replaced the wellingtons with grey knitted slippers that looked like enormous baby's bootees, and the mac with a grey cardigan. 'You'd better come into the kitchen. It's the only warm room in the house.'

'Where's your husband?'

Margaret looked back at her. 'He's in hospital. A stroke. I'm on my own here now.' She led the way down a corridor with a flag-stone floor. 'I'm selling up. The whole caboodle. Some London banker is interested. He pictures weekend house parties for his wealthy friends. Downton Abbey might be crap TV but it's done me no harm. All those city dwellers want to live the Edwardian dream.'

The kitchen was large and didn't seem very much warmer than the rest of the house. There was a chipped range with a scuttle of coke beside it. Margaret took the upright chair right next to the fire and nodded for Vera to sit at the table.

'How did you know Edward Forbes?'

'He's lived in Grindon for years.'

'What were you doing at his house this afternoon?' Vera thought this woman might be eccentric but she wasn't stupid. She was giving nothing away.

'He'd invited me to afternoon tea.'

To meet me? What was that about?

'Was that usual?'

Margaret gave a sharp, thin smile. 'Occasionally he took pity on me. I can't really look after myself – never had to until recently – and he could cook like a Michelin-starred chef.'

'Did you go inside this afternoon? Before you knocked on the Land Rover window?'

There was a brief moment of hesitation. 'No. I saw him through the conservatory window. As you did.'

Vera thought that would easily be checked. Margaret had been wearing gloves when Vera first saw her but those wellingtons would have been muddy and would have distinctive prints. Unless of course she'd taken them off before going inside.

Margaret turned towards Vera. 'Do you think someone killed him? That it was murder?' Her voice incredulous.

'Would anyone have a reason?'

'Not me. He was probably my only friend.'

There was a silence. 'Why do you think Edward wanted us to meet?' Vera said.

'I don't know. He didn't mention that he'd asked you. He phoned me this morning, rather excited. *Come along to tea, Maggie. I'll do one of my coffee and walnut cakes.*'

The woman imitated Forbes' voice: high-pitched, a little camp. The portrayal was so accurate that Vera had another jolt of memory. She was a teenager again, outside his cottage, listening to the adult conversation inside. Forbes was speaking, becoming angry and self-righteous. What was he saying? Something about starlings. She realized that Margaret was staring at her, waiting for another question.

'Did you know my father?' The question came out before Vera had time to think about it. 'Hector Stanhope.'

'You're Hector's daughter?' A little smile of surprise. And something else. Pity? 'I knew the family of course. We moved in the same circles when I was a girl. Hector was older than me. Always rather the black sheep.' Another smile. 'We all fancied him like mad. Then he married that little girl from the village. Not quite what his family expected.'

'She was a teacher. In the primary school.'

'Was she?' Margaret still seemed lost in memory. 'Where is old Hector now?'

'Dead.'

'Ah, I suppose he would be.' Margaret closed her eyes and began to hum a tune that Vera didn't recognize.

In the house in the hills that had once been Hector's Vera drank coffee with a glug of Scotch tipped in. The consensus from her colleagues was that Forbes had probably killed himself. They admitted it was weird that he'd obviously been expecting guests and had made preparations for tea: the coffee cake on the wire tray waiting to be iced, the scones still uncooked and ready for the oven. But he was elderly, a retired book keeper, lonely. Eccentric. There'd been no sign of forced entry. And the shot gun lying on the floor had belonged to the dead man.

Vera lit a fire and heated up a pan of soup left by her hippy neighbour. The sky was clear and later there would be the first frost of the winter. She tried to hear again in her head Margaret's imitation of Forbes' words to trigger more memory.

'A man has died.' Forbes' voice had been shrill and strained. It had taken him an effort to speak out.

'It was an accident.' Hector, trying to be patient. 'And really, what did he have to live for? No family. No work and no prospect of work.

Not where he came from.' It was Hector as she'd most despised him. Pompous and dismissive.

'*You can't talk about people like that!*' Forbes again. Vera closed her eyes and remembered. She'd heard Forbes walking to the window and knew that he must be looking outside. But he'd not seen her because she'd been standing too close to the cottage wall, away from his line of sight. '*As if they're not individuals. As if they're no more...*' he'd paused '*...than those starlings.*'

After that the conversation had become more heated, but Vera's memory faded and she couldn't conjure up the scene again.

The next morning in the office she checked the records for any suspicious death that had been reported at the time of the argument between Hector and Forbes. Nothing. Then it occurred to her that if the death had been connected with stolen eggs or young raptors it would have happened earlier in the year. No birds would be breeding in November. She came across the information first online and then she dug out the hard copy: a file about an infamous family from the west end of Newcastle. The Marlowes. There were still Marlowes causing bother in the town. Robbie Marlowe, aged nineteen, had been killed in a climbing accident. Some mountain in the Lake District. A long-forgotten detective had scrawled across the top of the report: *One less of the bastards to worry about.* Vera muttered under her breath: 'fewer not less'. Hector had been a stickler for grammar.

She remembered hearing about Robbie Marlowe when she first joined the force. He'd become a legend. According to colleagues he'd been a good-looking boy, charming, with expensive tastes. He'd been brought up to be a thief but in any other family he might have done well. He'd had brains. A cop she respected had said Robbie could have been in advertising. He could con any pensioner from her life savings. Or a barrister performing to an audience. He'd been a city lad. His haunts had been the clubs and pubs of Newcastle. Vera couldn't imagine that any of the Marlowe family would be into outdoor pursuits, so what had Robbie been doing halfway up a rope in the Cumbria fells? The answer came easily. She'd recognised the name of the place and could picture it on a map and in the landscape. A steep cliff by the side of a reservoir near Keswick. Hector had taken her there one day but decided that the climb was beyond him. It was a breeding site for peregrine falcons.

Things clicked into place very quickly then. Hector had hired Robbie to collect the eggs for him. The boy had fallen to his death. It had been an accident of sorts but provoked by her father. And months later, on a cold November afternoon Edward Forbes had plucked up courage to confront Hector. *'You treat people as if they are no more than these starlings.'*

And now, according to Edward Forbes' letter, it was happening all over again. People were being treated as if they had no rights, as if they were no more than common birds. Vera leaned back in her chair and let her brain, her imagination and her memory pick through the details of the case.

She found Margaret Lawlor outside, raking dead leaves from the lawn in front of the house. The same wellingtons but an army great coat instead of the mackintosh.

'It'll take you a while to clear all this, mind.'

Margaret scooped the leaves into an ancient wheelbarrow, and stretched. She was still holding the rake. 'What do you want?'

'A chat.' Vera was tempted to add: about the starlings. 'This banker that's buying the estate, what's he planning to do with it?'

'I told you.' Margaret's voice was contemptuous. 'He wants to play squire for his friends. At the weekends at least.'

'You still own a bit of the hill at the back of Grindon.' A statement not a question. 'They used to shoot there in your father's day.' Hector had turned out as beater when times were hard. 'I dare say that would have appealed to your young banker. The idea of a shooting party. Taking a few brace of grouse back as gifts to show off to his city colleagues.'

Margaret said nothing.

'Still employ a gamekeeper do you?' Vera's words were hard. Bitter.

'I'm not sure what business that is of yours, Inspector.' Margaret Lawlor stared out into the distance. The wind blew her white hair away from her face.

'I'm sure he comes as part of the package with the house. The old family retainer in his tied cottage. As you said, Downton Abbey has a lot to answer for.'

Margaret said nothing and Vera continued. 'But there are hen harriers breeding on the hill. Taking the grouse. That might have upset things. Probably not a deal-breaker actually. Your city banker probably wouldn't know a harrier if it bit him. But you weren't taking any chances, were you? You need this sale to go through. Best put some poison down to get rid. The harriers are only vermin in your eyes after all.'

'I deserve some comfort in my old age!' It was a return of the fighting spirit.

'Of course it's against the law to poison hen harriers.' Now Vera kept her voice calm and reasonable. She could see an end to this. 'And you would never break the law, would you? Not Margaret Lawlor who sat on the bench for thirty years dishing out justice. But your gamekeeper. That would be a different story. What did you tell him? That he was in danger of losing his cottage and his livelihood if the sale didn't go through.' *Treating him as if he has no more rights than the starlings.*

'It's my land. I should be able to do as I please with it.' The wind blew a flurry of icy rain across the garden but the women didn't move.

'Then Edward Forbes found out what was going on and it troubled his conscience. He wrote to me and invited me to tea. He wanted me to meet you. Perhaps he hoped I might be able to talk some sense into you.'

'I did not kill that man.' It came out as a self-righteous bellow.

'You didn't need to. Your gamekeeper had killed birds for you. How did you persuade him to kill a man? Did you promise him a big bonus if the sale went through? There was nothing explicit of course. Mrs. Justice Lawlor couldn't bring herself to hire a hitman.'

The silence stretched. 'If that's all, Inspector, I'll get back to work.' Margaret remained quite still, holding the rake in her hand.

'But you had to check,' Vera said. 'You had to make sure Edward Forbes was dead. And besides he'd invited you to tea. He was your only friend.' When she continued she spoke almost in a whisper. 'What did you see when you saw him through the window? Were you pleased he'd been killed? Or had you hoped, deep down, that it hadn't happened? That your keeper had developed some sense. That we'd drink tea and eat cake and make polite conversation.'

Margaret seemed about to answer but she only shook her head. Driving back to Kimmerston Vera stopped to watched the starlings putting on a show for her. Thousands of individual birds formed intricate patterns over her vehicle. Then they disappeared over the horizon and were lost to sight.

MOUNTAINS OUT OF MOLEHILLS

VALERIE LAWS

Summer, 1970s

The pigs were so big, so threatening as they milled about in their open enclosure, naked-looking and grubby. Ian had never seen pigs close up before, thought of them as pink, chubby, greedy and good-natured. These had long lean bodies, powerful shoulders, massive heads with bristling ears, small pale eyes.

'We're away after woodies!' Huw had grabbed an Aztec bar from the hostel shop without breaking stride. 'Want to come along?'

Ian felt torn, going shooting with the lads – he who loved wildlife, going out killing. But he also loved feeling part of the Welsh farmer lads' world of carefree lawlessness, of this landscape, so he went, in Dewi's mud-splashed Landrover, wishing his mates at Uni or back home could see him now. All the local lads had guns, knives, and Dewi even wore a slim silver axe in his belt. It was like the Wild West; the Wild West of Wales. Today they were after wood pigeons, and Y Garn farm was a good place to find them, attracted by spilled grain. They were fun to shoot, moving targets taking off with a rattling of wings. Ian had rescued an injured pigeon once. But this was a rite of passage, of belonging.

So he followed the four lads as they quietly padded into the yard, shotguns over their shoulders, their double barrels' beady eyes looking back at him. He was relieved to see the guns were 'broken' as per proper procedure. He knew about stuff like that now he was a real countryman. When Doug, his boss for the summer, went out with them, he'd forget and Ian once found himself walking right behind him... what if Doug tripped? Ian secretly practiced shooting baked bean tins with an old airgun. He had a bruise on his forehead where the kickback bit him, but he hoped to be offered a turn with a shotgun one day. Scanning for woodies, gun barrels now snapped-to, the lads ignored the nearby pigs barging about, restless and excited.

'There!' A frantic fusillade of wings as the desperate birds climbed the air, then the blasting of guns, terrifyingly loud. Ian, standing close, was deafened, his ears ringing. The lads, lanky drawling Dewi, pretty rich boy Huw and even prettier Daf, all tall blonds typical of this former Viking stronghold, and dark, stocky Idris were totally caught up in the killing, eyes alight. Birds tumbled as feathers took off, and one plump pigeon crashed down among the pigs. To Ian's horror they fought over it, squealing with unholy joy. Dead or dying, or just winged, it didn't matter, it vanished, a pearly grey, reddening puff of smoke under the indecent slablike bodies.

'Aye, no use tryin to beat the pigs to a pigeon, they love em,' Idris shouted to Ian, amused.

'Pigs eat meat?' Ian yelled back, still partly deafened.

'They'll eat anythin, pigs,' said Daf. 'They'd eat yew, if yew fell in there!' He playfully levelled his shotgun at Ian and mimed shooting him into the pen. Ian flinched.

Laughing, the four exchanged banter in Welsh as they gathered up the limp birds. Of course Daf had been joking, but the feeding frenzy was disturbing. Looking dazedly into the pen, Ian suddenly felt faint, fear of the pigs' blunt tusky teeth and pungent heft made him back off, but not before he'd noticed a shirt button just inside the enclosure wall, like the ones on his cheesecloth shirt. Could..? But no, that was just something the farmer or his workers had dropped. How would they handle the pigs if they were that dangerous?

'Here.' Huw held out his shotgun to Ian. 'Have a go.' His intensely blue eyes were friendly. This was significant – an acknowledgement that Ian was one of them now, could even, perhaps, literally be one of them, because of Megan, Huw's younger sister. Ian's holiday romance was innocent but intense. She was a bit young for him, so it was all romantic hand-holding, earnest conversations and goodnight kisses. Even if he'd felt inclined to push his luck – and she was pretty in a soft, Scandinavian sort of way – during their kisses he kept his hands in check. Despite their enviably early losses of virginity, the lads had strong opinions about blokes who messed about with their sisters.

'You wanna watch yourself mate,' Doug had said, 'Dewi's sister was jilted by a lad from Wolverhampton, well they were all out looking for him with their shotguns loaded, oh, he was lucky to get off Pen Caer alive. Never been back since.'

But Huw and his pals seemed all in favour as they teased Ian about his evening trysts with Megan down the flower-garlanded lane, which made him feel even more like he belonged. He imagined staying in this spectacular, wild, beautiful place, working mostly outdoors instead of moving to London to start his graduate trainee job at Midland Bank with its immense £3,000 per annum starting salary which he'd gained on the university 'milk round' but which now seemed a dull prospect. Megan shared his fantasy, talking in her soft south-Walian accent about a farming future together, entrancing and beguiling as any mythic Celtic maiden.

This was more real than any bank, holding her brother's hot, heavy gun, waiting for a target. Ian lifted the heavy barrels, and slowly turned, the faces of the lads succeeding each other in his sights, Dewi, Idris, Daf, Huw... straining to keep the gun steady, he kept the sights on Huw who seemed suddenly very clear yet far away and small. He could marry Megan, learn Welsh (he already managed greetings, and orders at the Siop: caws, afalau, bara...), though Huw would inherit the family farm tucked under Garn Fawr...

Huw's hand came out to take the gun back, possessive.

'No woodies now, man.' Daf lit a cigarette.

'Never mind,' Idris said, 'next time, eh.'

The four lads lit up Embassy Regals Doug bought cheap from the Cash 'n' Carry. Although it hadn't been a real turn with the gun, Ian felt like the divide between him and them, him and Pen Caer, was as thin and fragile as cigarette paper.

The Welsh do kind of make mountains out of molehills, Ian thought, as he stood on top of Garn Fawr, 'Great Mountain.' Like other Garns, it was really little more than a glowering rocky hill, squatting on the spectacular cliffs. But its apparent height was greatly extended by the sheer drop from the cliff top down to a tiny almost inaccessible rocky beach and the shimmering turquoise waves. Sweat dried on his skin in the hot breeze, the bronzed sun beginning its slow, glorious descent into the sea. Insects droned, dodging the spiders' silvery hammocks swagged over the gorse. Stonechats perched on thistle tops, clicking like the stone tools of those who first lived here.

Ian liked to scramble up the Garn every evening, when his job of baking frozen steak and kidney pies was done, the apple crumble (tinned apples, crumble mix) served in catering trays. Living in the real countryside, he'd learned, meant convenience food. Fresh veg was hard to get, ironically, apart from the sacks of new local spuds they got hostellers to scrape by the ton. Tomorrow was Angel Delight day. Even now, six weeks into his summer job, he felt a childish thrill mixing huge bowls of it (catering packs, just add water), and eating as much as he liked.

As he gazed down on the dazzling sugar-cube hostel, perched between Garn and cliff edge, he saw a cream Mini shoot too fast down the drive, to halt just short of the wall. Ian knew Huw was driving his

Mam's mini because he'd just written off his Cortina. The lads were younger than Ian but as well as guns and knives, they had cars, and most of all, they had sex, plenty of it. The irony that he, a student in these permissive 70s, should have had such slim pickings compared to these boys, active from about thirteen, casually doing 'what you shouldn't' between car crashes and shooting anything that moved! While he'd kept getting off at Hall of Residence discos with nice girls who clung to church and mummy's good advice; why was that? Hi ho, where was the silver lining? Even this summer, with all the lusty wenches in shorts brushing past in the hostel corridor, he'd ended up with Megan, another 'good girl'.

Still, the lads had accepted Ian as a friend. Even though they spoke Welsh among themselves, they moved easily between languages and he didn't feel left out. But it was strange how little they seemed to appreciate the countryside or their rich heritage. The young farmers never walked if they could drive, and drove everywhere like madmen. They ate frozen food, smoked, drank Bacardi, talked guns, cars and combines. And girls of course, the ever-renewed supply of holiday-loosened talent luring them as soon as work was done. Girls, and Mars Bars. They ran up shop tabs longer than the Pembrokeshire Coast Path. He couldn't see Huw go in to the hostel but he saw Dewi's Landrover lurching down the drive. Ian knew why the lads were turning up sooner and faster than usual these days: Susi, the new assistant, was now installed, and they were competing for her attention. He smiled, for once feeling superior to the lads on their own terms.

Susi had burst into his life like a shotgun cartridge, shattering his calm, bringing a hot peppering of sex to the bland diet he'd been existing on while his parents' generation moaned about student immorality. He didn't care what they thought, it felt damn good. God she was sexy. And experienced. She'd taught him a thing or two already, and it had only been one night. Now he had something to boast about to the lads, all good-looking, experienced rollers in hay, though a bit young for Susi, but she'd picked Ian to wrap her slim legs around. But he couldn't tell them. Everyone knew everything on Pen Caer it was said, but not this, he hoped. Of course he wasn't technically two-timing Megan, they weren't actually boy- and girl-friend, as they weren't sleeping together. And Susi was obviously casual about sex, they'd only been working together a few days and she'd dragged him off to her narrow straw mattress in her tiny cubby hole partitioned off from the girl's dorm. Lucky it was hostel closed night! Oh wow it was good... and all thanks to the cows.

Last night, as he and Susi organised the hostellers' packed lunches, he'd tried not to look too obviously at her clinging cotton zip-up top though he'd longed to pull the zip down. He could tell she wasn't wearing a bra. Definitely a women's libber. Friendly, approachable, but he didn't dare try anything. He had to work with her in the hot sweaty kitchen all summer vac after all. But then late last night really had been like the Wild West. They were all asleep when the phone rang, he could just hear it from his attic and surfaced to hear Doug rapping on the attic hatch.

'Come on, young Ian', he'd rasped amid smoker's coughing, 'Dewi's cows are out!'

Bewildered, Ian stumbled down the ladder, and out into the pitch black night where the stars hung down like silver fruit, following Doug's torch into the hostel Landrover, Susi too, swift and easy in her movements, her eyes in the darkness shining with adventure. In no time, they were down one of Pen Caer's narrow lanes bordered by high, turfed stone walls with hedges on top. Dewi's dad hoisted a five-barred metal gate off its hinges and positioned it across the road further down.

'Here, darlin'', he said, grabbing Susi by the shoulders and positioning her behind the free-standing gate. 'Hold this gate up, see, in case the buggers come charging down this way when we chase them out, and DON'T let them past you, right?' and they left her standing there, alone in the dark, slight and small behind the grid of the gate she was propping up to fend off a herd of stampeding cattle. Ian offered to help her but he was hauled off to the field where the cows belonged, its open gate opposite the field where they were now gorging themselves on dangerous crops, like the sheep in 'Far From the Madding Crowd'. He heard engines labouring behind the high hedges, panicked mooing, and the lads' wild whoops, presumably using Landrovers to round up the cows as he'd seen them dazzle rabbits at night, when they'd take turns to be the shooter sitting in the spare tyre on the bonnet.

'Get you into this field, lad, and when the cows are all back in, you shut the gate quick, right?' and Dewi's dad was off. Ian stood in the dark, as the sounds grew louder and he heard the clatter of hooves on the asphalt lane, now getting fainter. Poor Susi!

Then her voice shouting, 'Yah, yah, go on, yah!' and they charged back up and into their field, a black tide of snorting, barging shapes, and Ian swung the gate shut, remembering just in time to be on the outside of it, and then all the helpers were laughing and chatting, high on the adventure and the night. Susi was all lit up, but still dead cool, her faded flared jeans and zip-up top sexier than any fancy outfit, as the lads were clearly aware, while she treated them like younger brothers.

But later when she and Ian were alone on the hostel drive, still buzzing, she put her hand on his arm, 'Look!' at a shooting star arcing over them and suddenly they were kissing, really snogging, and her tongue slid into his mouth like a shot of Southern Comfort, and it was happening, like an X-rated film, and he was pulling down that zip...

And today it hadn't been awkward at all, but why should it be, she'd not expect them to be going steady or anything, she wasn't a good girl like Megan... Megan was young, innocent, she'd be hurt if he stopped seeing her, and why should he. He could have sex with Susi, god he hoped she'd still want to, and romance with Megan. He could have it both ways for once, fantasise about living here with the wild peregrines and the cliffs and the Garn. This was a magic place, where things happened but didn't somehow touch you, like the lads writing off their cars, pinning up local newspaper cuttings of the wrecks, boasting about it, without a scratch on them.

Ian's summer went on being magical. He was intoxicated with Susi, desperate for her in ways he'd never thought possible. She seemed wild for him, the chemistry was amazing, but he went on seeing Megan down the lane each evening after his Garn scramble, holding hands and kissing chastely. He was a bit fed up with it to be honest but couldn't face breaking up with her, the hurt in her soft blue eyes, and to cover up his boredom he talked even more about how much he loved Pen Caer, and how they could have a little farm... or he could work on her dad's farm... or Doug couldn't be far from retirement...

His limbs felt light and strong from his nights and afternoons with Susi in his attic or her cubbyhole when the hostellers were out, he could run up Garn Fawr lightly, barely out of breath, run down again and on, more slowly down, down the steep narrow cliff path, little more than a tiny shelf sticking out from the sheer cliff face, down to the little rocky beach where no holiday makers went, skim a stone or two, or lock eyes with a seal popping its dog-like head curiously above the water, and then he'd climb back to the cliff top, feeling the pull of the muscles in his thighs, often carrying with him a piece of driftwood, long planks sometimes which the sea tossed ashore and which, Doug told him, could hurt the baby seals left there during Autumn high tides. He used the planks as shelves propped up on stones, now Susi shared the attic, though they still kept it from Doug, and Ian had never felt so much a man. He may not have a shotgun, but he had something a lot better now. The lads hung out at the hostel, with Ian, Susi and Doug, though it was clear Dewi fancied Susi more than a bit. On one of the hostel closed nights they drank too much Cash 'n' Carry vodka and orange squash. Ian passed out, the lads slept anywhere and he had a suspicion one of them, Dewi perhaps, might have tried, or even succeeded, in sleeping in the same room as Susi, which made him feel ill with jealousy, but he had nothing to go on and no real right to be possessive. There was no change in the affectionate, teasing, flirty/matey relationship between Susi and any of the lads. Ian and Susi would go down to the tiny beach in the hot afternoon sometimes, swim in the chilly Atlantic, have sex in the sea, sheltered from view by the almost invisible path and the overhanging cliff.

One night, on his usual solo trip, Ian struggled up the cliff with a wide plank, bark still on its edges, being careful to balance as he went up the perilously narrow path, especially the eroded bit near the top, where gorse roots seemed to be all that held up a few feet of the path and he could feel it give slightly beneath his feet. When he was with Susi, they'd make sure to pass this part separately, lightly stepping over it, but they weren't scared. It was all part of the adventure, the magic of this place where cars flew harmlessly through the air.

Now he carried his prize into the hostel in sweaty triumph, looked into the kitchen and stopped in his tracks. A rabbit's head sat on the bench, looking at him with gluey eyes, next to its pink gutted body. Susi stood there red to the wrists, holding the skin like a furry little sweater in one hand, a big bloody knife in the other.

'Hi,' she said casually, 'Huw brought this so I'm doing rabbit in cider in the Aga for our dinner.'

Ian felt dizzy suddenly, probably just the climb carrying the heavy plank, but it reminded him of the pigs and the pigeon.

'Look,' Susi's dark eyes seemed feral and sparky, her high cheekbones tribal, 'she was pregnant. Poor little things.' She pointed to what looked like raw kidneys on the bench, embryo rabbits, curled and dead.

Ian and Susi never showed each other affection outside the bedroom anyway, but he felt completely alien for a moment. Then he shook it off. He'd eaten rabbit before in a restaurant in France, and he'd eat it tonight. And then later... He felt lust surge in his grubby jeans and a joyful triumph. He wanted to show her he was as much a man as any of the lads. Huw could bring her a dead bunny, he'd do something better. He stood the plank on end, taller than him.

'Another shelf?' she laughed. 'I think we've got enough of those!'

'Oh, just helping the seals you know,' he said.

Susi did strange things to him, he had strange feelings around her, but of course it couldn't be love. He and Susi were all about sex. She

didn't have feelings apart from friendliness, he was sure. Susi knew
he met Megan down the lane, she couldn't fail to, as the lads and
Doug joked about it every evening. She mustn't mind. She'd never
said anything. He'd still feel a bit guilty, somehow, felt impelled to say
he'd rather not see Megan but you know, very young, easily hurt, he'd
have to let her down lightly, and of course they all knew she'd just had
bad exam results as well, not got the grades for uni or even poly, so it
wasn't the time...

In time it became more and more clear from the subtly changing
colours of the bracken, the slow shift from mainly green to gold and
umber, that summer was running out. Ian began to contemplate his
move to London and new well-paid career with more favour. Megan
presumably didn't know about Susi. But his situation with the two
girls was stifling and worrying, and this menial job cooking suppers
and cleaning the hostel and helping out on the nearby farms had
less appeal now he'd had a proper break from years of school and
academic work. Novelty worn off, boredom set in. He still loved Pen
Caer, the coast path, the Garn and the sea, of course, but he seemed to
be emerging from some sort of summer spell. He couldn't imagine not
seeing or touching Susi, or sharing his bed with her, but she'd get over it
and so would he. He'd have a new confidence now, shame he'd not had
it at uni, he could probably have had some of the popular cool girls.
He'd have to break up with Megan too. She'd have to understand
that all his talk of staying here was really just fantasy. These people
had no ambition – looking around, he saw those only a few years
older than the lads and their sisters, already paunchy from too many
Aztecs and Curly Wurlys, yellow-toothed from smoking, doing the
same things year in, year out. Megan had no ambition either, hadn't

even seemed that upset about her exam results, about staying on Pen Caer helping on the farm or getting a crappy job instead of going to university. But maybe in a few years, as a successful banker, he'd buy the old cottage tucked in below the Garn, do it up. He'd come back for summer holidays with his wife. Or come alone, meet up with Susi for some illicit hanky panky as his mistress, though she said nothing after he'd made this suggestion to her. Sometimes he'd recall her bloody hands, her shining eyes, the knife, the slit rabbit, but no, she was cool. She'd be cool with them parting ways. Yet he felt some primitive need to give her a gift, almost like an offering to a dangerous goddess, or maybe just to make the parting less cold.

So when on his last evening, with the lads all gathered round, Susi was saying how much she wanted the massive plank they'd found on the beach, he inwardly resolved to bring it up the cliff; Dewi's promise to go get it for her as soon as he could stiffened his determination. Not only was it big and thick, but made of beautiful, reddish wood much denser and heavier than normal. He and Susi had tried carrying it but given up, though he was sure he was strong enough now despite the narrow path. She coveted the fashionable 'refectory' table in Daf's parents' farm kitchen. Doug said he could saw it in two, join the pieces edge to edge, use driftwood to make the trestles and bar.

And so later, Ian did his last Garn Fawr climb and cliff descent. The evening before, he'd ended his embarrassingly childish romance with Megan. Awkward. He'd been a bit nervous; the lads, especially Huw, wouldn't be friends with him any more, not that it mattered much now. However, Huw had invited him to go shooting with them early next morning at the pig farm before he left in the afternoon. So no hard feelings.

He set off down the narrow shelf of cliff path, careful as always, clinging to the cliffside, especially at the dodgy little bit with the springy netting of gorse roots under his feet. Concentrating took his mind off guilt at Megan's quiet acceptance of his departure, like a stoical hurt animal, her eyes shining with tears. Down on the tideline he lifted one end of the heavy plank, dragging it laboriously over the rocks towards the path, with rest stops. A huge bull seal watched him with interest from the sea. This would be a real challenge. He began to work his zigzag way slowly up the cliff, pushing the plank ahead of him, pulling it after him, until the path got too narrow for that and he made the supreme effort, glorying in his strong arms and back and legs, hoisting up the plank under his arm, bracing with the other arm, leaning inwards against the cliff as he slowly staggered up. He could always drop it if he had to, but he was determined to make it. Every muscle hurt and sweat ran into his eyes but he felt good. He was a man, challenged in his manliness. He had had two girlfriends. Two, at the same time! He was leaving them behind. He had farmer friends who'd accepted him as one of themselves. He had prospects. Choices. He reached the narrowest, most eroded part of the path. He could do it, even with the weight of the plank. He stepped onto the dodgy bit and his foot went through it, dropping him down, encumbered by the plank, confused, clutching at some scraps of grass and gorse which stabbed his clinging hands. Ian had to let the plank go thud, thudding down from rock to rock, returning to the sea.

'Ian!'

He looked up, relief coursing through him. Dewi's tanned face looked down at him with those bright blue eyes. 'Come on mate!' He was lying on the cliff top, his whole chest and belly now over the edge, lowering his axe handle to pull him up. Ian reached for the axe, his foot lodged on a small nub of gorse root which was already pulling free. He grabbed at it, his sweaty fingers slipping on its cold metal surface, feeling the shreds of gorse giving way beneath him, feeling his guts turn to water, Dewi's face a blur through the sweat in his eyes.

'Help me! Dewi help!'

Earth clods rattled down taking the path with them.

'Sorry Ian. But you broke Megan's heart, messed her life up proper.'

Megan? Ian tried to think as he clung on. 'I never touched her! It was Susi I slept with...' but he felt the axe handle slip from his fingers, and something hard smash into his skull, bringing blackness but not yet oblivion, as he fell to the rock-pounded waves far below.

Dewi called the coastguard on his CB radio. There was no sign of Ian now, though there was a red splash and something else on a rocky ledge about halfway down. Those gorse roots had been tough buggers, and he'd not had long while Ian was up Garn Fawr. He'd known the extra weight of the plank would make all the difference on the weakened path, known Ian wouldn't be able to resist the challenge. He and Huw would repair the path, it was only right. He'd quite liked Ian, and Megan had been stupid, turning down her uni place at Leeds, lying about her results, because she'd thought Ian was staying. Messing up her prospects, now sobbing her heart out that it was all for nothing. She'd have been the first person on Pen Caer to go to University, do anything but farming at college, not that Dewi could see the point of it really.

But Huw had helped him when that bastard broke his sister's heart, and Dewi was honour bound to return the favour. He'd almost decided to let Ian off with a bad scare, but the idea of Ian screwing Susi – stringing Megan along – no, that was too much. Not much of a risk, really – if anyone had seen anything, it would be him trying to save Ian from falling.

And Susi might be back next year.

He waited for the coastguard, cleaning his axe on the tussocky grass as Garn Fawr gazed down on the creamy green sea and the choughs wheeled, calling, as they always had and always would.

PORT LION

MARGARET MURPHY

The estuary looks bigger now the tide is out.

I notice the little streams and ditches carved by the river, rowing boats beached in the mud, rocks humped like burial mounds, cold light shivering off the salt water moating their bases. Further out – it seems so much further, now – the receding tide forms a lake, reflecting a mirage of sky and the distant woods.

Before, it was all water, just a few boats bobbing on it, and its sameness made it seem smaller. But the ebb tide's slow revelation of mud and rocks, sand and seaweed reveals the distance, how far I have gone.

Parallel lines scar the sand, like experimental cuts on a suicide's wrist. A fanciful notion that; some might say morbid – after all, they're only gouge marks where the waves have lifted and dropped, lifted and dropped, lifted... and stranded the little fishing boats.

The salt-marsh stink of seaweed and samphire is sharpened by tumbled shellfish ripped from the mud by last night's storm. Clusters of empty dog-whelk cases skitter across the mud like popped bubble-wrap. The sun-warmed land summons an onshore breeze which carries a new, subtle note to me, at once sweeter and more poignant on the nose. A low whimper rises in my throat.

A mist hovers between the sea and the land, drawing a grey line in the sand, and through it, three spectral figures bend like cocklers over the mud. The sun, refracted through the mist, magnifies the hunched figures, pulling that distant spot into the foreground, so that it isn't there anymore, it's here. And when one of the figures stands straight and stares inland, it feels like they are staring right at me.

An unseen oystercatcher sends up a quick, piping call and the alarm is taken up by another, and another, and another, until the air seems alive with it. Suddenly they appear, a black arrow speeding low over the mudflat; the thrum of wings and the burble and piping of a hundred frightened birds racing ahead of the flock. Abruptly, they turn, soaring up in an arc, reversing direction, a swirl of smoke against the pale sky. The distant figures, distracted by the burst of noise and movement, raise their heads to watch, and I take my chance to slip away.

'You haven't been swimming in the Daugleddau?'

The Daugleddau is the meeting place of the two Cleddau rivers, and this is Mrs Jenkins, swaddled in jersey and resplendent in yellow, her pinkish hair a counterpoint, suggestive of her own rhubarb pudding. In high season she welcomes fine young men into the bosom of her home, and is warmed by their proximity. In low season, she retreats, devoting herself to embroidery and her two Balinese cats, chosen on account of their clownish good nature – and her allergies. Mrs Jenkins is a martyr to her sinuses.

'You shouldn't go swimming in those waters.' She looks at the three of us as if we are her own dear boys, her eyes wide with anxiety. 'It's not safe.'

'I've been wild swimming in Snowdonia and the Brecon Beacons, Mrs Jenkins,' Adam says, shooting a smug glance at me and Graham. 'I've swum the length of Bala, four miles nose to tail, jumped the blue lagoon at Abereiddy – I even survived a riptide off Castle Beach in Tenby.' He flashes her the smile he usually reserves for his girlfriends' mothers. 'Half man, half cork, that's me.'

'Oh, I can see that – ' Mrs Jenkins blushes soft and peachy, like the girl she must have been twenty years before, and Adam gives me a look that says, What can you do? 'Not the cork bit,' she says. 'I meant you've got a swimmer's build. It's not the tides I'm on about, Adambach,' Mrs Jenkins says, thoughtfully gathering up our empty dinner plates. 'Though they do have a part in the story.'

The story. I lean forward, willing her to go on.

But she digresses. 'You don't ever want to get caught on an ebbing tide on the Daugleddau. My Melvyn went that way. Fishing in a rowboat on Cleddau Ddu, swept out on a spring tide's ebb. Capsized in Milford Haven.' She sighs over the dirty dishes.

Adam checks his watch, ready to call time and Graham shoots me a panicky look. She can't stop there. He jerks his chin, willing me to take charge.

I can't think of anything else to say, so I blurt out 'But what about the legend?'

She looks at me, startled, and Adam bugs his eyes at me like he's Mister Sensitive all of a sudden.

'Sorry, Mrs Jenkins,' I say. 'It's just I'm really into myths and legends – the Mabinogion, all that stuff – '

'Oh, this is not what you'd call a legend,' she says, 'Just a local tale, really.' But her face has brightened and she places our knives and forks neatly on top of the stack of plates, taking her time; all she wants is a little more persuasion.

Graham takes my lead: 'He's mad for stories – what d'you call it – '

'Oral tradition,' I say, and Adam sniggers.

Graham glares at him, still talking to her: 'It's true – he even dragged us up the Preseli Mountains to see King Arthur's Grave,' he says.

'Bedd Arthur.' Mrs Jenkins clasps her hands across her broad middle. 'Now there's a legend.'

'But folk tales are the best,' I say, and it's like I plucked the words right out of her head.

She shunts the dishes to one side, settles her wide beam back in the chair, and rests her elbows on the table, her dark eyes agleam.

Adam clears his throat and taps his watch. Drinking time wasting. Graham frowns at him and I avoid his gaze. Finally he subsides.

'It all began at Llangwm, a mile or so up the road from here,' Mrs Jenkins says. 'During my great-great-grandmother's girlhood, it was. Lilith Yates was a lovely girl, black-haired and rosy-cheeked – had the pick of any man from here to Haverfordwest – it was just bad luck she fell for Dylan Hews.' Her mouth twists as she says the name. 'Lived in the end house, a finger's width from Cleddau Ddu – meaning Black Cleddau. Dylan liked fishing for sport; moored his own little rowboat six feet from his own garden gate. A picket fence and a foot of marsh grass all they had to keep the river at bay.

'Now, Dylan always had a restless eye for the ladies – and Lilith put up with his dalliances for years, forgiving him, making excuses, taking it all on herself. Most of the girls dropped Dylan before he ever got bored with them. Until he took up with golden-haired Anwen, as pretty as her name, but with a stone cold heart brimful of wickedness.

'Together, the lovers plotted to do away with Lilith. One night, with the two rivers in full swell and the rain lashing hard enough to drown a duck, Dylan slips a sleeping draught into Lilith's cocoa and him and Anwen lower his poor wife into the boat. He rows out to the Daugleddau where the Black Cleddau and the White Cleddau meet, and Dylan and his lover tip Lilith into water as the tide turns.

'Maybe it was the shock of the cold, or maybe Dylan didn't give her enough of the sleeping draught; whatever the reason, Lilith wakes and with a fearful cry begs her husband to save her. Anwen snatches up an oar and pushes her away and they row for home, soon losing sight of her in the crow-black sea. But as they are about to turn a bend in the river, the clouds part and a full moon shines on the water and there, in the turbulent meeting of the rivers, Dylan sees his poor wife waving to him, pleading for him to come back to her.' She pauses. 'Lilith's body was found in Milford Haven harbour a week later.'

Graham and me sink back in our chairs, but Adam wants to know more. 'How did they get caught?' he says.

'Who says they did?' Graham says.

'They must have – or we wouldn't be listening to the story, would we?'

'Oh, but they weren't caught,' Mrs Jenkins says. 'Not at first, anyway – as a matter of fact, nobody suspected a thing. There was a coroner's inquest: Dylan claimed Lilith must have sleepwalked into the river, said he'd rescued her once before. Her mother agreed, she had been prone to sleepwalking since she was a girl. The verdict was accidental death.' She smiled grimly. 'But Dylan was haunted by the sight of gentle Lilith, sinking in the waves, her arms white in the moonlight, and the two murderers fell to quarrelling. People started to talk, and a second inquest was called. Anwen turned King's Evidence, and two months later Dylan was hanged for the murder of his wife. Two days after that, Anwen disappeared, lost overboard from a ferryboat, crossing the Cleddau Ddu at Pembroke Ferry. It was night-time, and a full moon, and all that night as they searched for Anwen there were sightings in the Daugleddau of a woman, her slim arms raised imploringly above the waves. Boats were sent out, but they found nothing. Some said it was Anwen, waving for help. But others swore that the creature in the river had raven black hair and her eyes seemed to burn with an unnatural light. To this day, Lilith is said to haunt the Daugleddau on moonlit nights, luring faithless souls to their deaths.'

'Nice,' Adam claps his hands, grinning broadly. 'But I got nothing to fear, Mrs J,' He winks and me and Graham. 'I'm between girlfriends at the moment.'

A police van and a Range Rover are parked up by the time I reach the patch of uneven concrete that serves as a car park. A cop in a suit – must be the one in charge – pulls on a pair of wellies and a wax jacket. Two more, both in uniform, are hitching a trailer to the back of the SUV. Graham is waiting for me, binoculars trained on the distant figures on the mudflat.

'It's him then,' I say.

'It's him. They're bringing him in before the tide turns.'

The Range Rover trundles down the slipway and out onto the mud, two cops and two crime scene types in white overalls on board.

We have already been questioned: out on the Black Cleddau for a moonlight swim, I told them, one in the boat, two in the water. It was Adam and Graham's turn to swim, dry suited, sensibly close to the shore. Adam said he saw someone in trouble – someone waving out where the two rivers meet – went to investigate. Graham tried to follow, got into difficulties. I rowed out to rescue him; hauled him, exhausted, into the boat. When I looked again, Adam had vanished.

We searched, but the storm blew up with sudden ferocity and we were forced ashore.

Mrs Jenkins will make a good witness: raised the alarm when we staggered into her kitchen, traumatised, soaking wet, poured tales of Adam's bravado and Lilith's sad end into the ears of the search and rescue party as she dispensed tea and Welsh cakes to sustain their efforts.

Graham and me watch the slow progress of the recovery operation out on the mudflat, sharing the binoculars and taking nips of whisky from Graham's hip flask.

'I suppose we should tell the girls,' I say. Our girlfriends are living La Vida Loca on the Costa del Sol for a week while we lads bond over watersports and hill climbing.

'They'll be awful cut up,' Graham says.

'Yeah, they will be,' I say as, out on the mud, two men in white overalls enlist help from the uniform cops to heft a body bag onto the trailer.

'Arrogant tosser,' Graham snorts. "Between girlfriends."

'Not anymore, he isn't,' I say, blocking that sordid little picture from my mind.

'This'll ruin the girls' holiday,' Graham says, training his bins on the Range Rover chugging back towards the slipway and dry land.

'Shame to spoil it for them,' I say. 'I'd prefer to see their faces when we give them the news. Wouldn't you?'

He grins, hands me the hip flask. 'You have all the best ideas.'

I take the flask, propose a toast to Lilith.

The sun has burned off the thin veil of mist in the distance, revealing the tracery of a ghost moon close to the horizon. Summer clouds scud across the sky as the last few cops trudge back over the mud, and the brackish water of the estuary dances with a million pinpricks of light.

I borrow Graham's field glasses and follow their progress for a few moments, then track backwards to the spot they just left. I see churned up mud, a marker of some kind with police ribbon cracking and spinning from it. I shift my focus to the 'lake' I saw half an hour before and can see from the raised perspective of the car park that it is, in fact, the mouth of the estuary. He didn't travel far at all – or perhaps he did, and then the river turned and brought him back again – the human cork, bobbing on the swell. The tide is on the turn and sea water spills onto the mudflat, already lapping at the bases of the humped rocks. Something moves right to left in my field of view – a flash of white. Heart pounding, I jerk the glasses back to the spot, but there is only the rapid jangle of sunlight reflected from the tips of the waves.

'What?' Graham asks.

'Nothing,' I say.

Reflections on the water, I tell myself, a dolphin out in the bay. That could be it. Yes, that's certainly it – the dazzle of sunlight on the waves, the flash of a fin – that, and the loss of a night's sleep.

But my eyes scour the shimmering water restlessly.

SORTED
TOBY
FORWARD

She just walked out on him.

They hadn't even had an argument, let alone a row.

The note she left was clear enough about what was happening, but gave no clue about why.

'I'm leaving. Don't follow me.'

Ben put the camera bag on the bed and checked the wardrobe, even though he knew what he was going to find. His things were there. Hers weren't.

No point in looking in the bathroom.

The room still smelled of her.

He loved that moment, early in the day, when the room was filled with scent. That was the thing about living with a woman. The world smelled better. One of the things, anyway.

He rang her mobile and shrugged when it went straight to voicemail.

She probably had a new one anyway. She was a planner and whatever it looked like, this was planned.

Three hours ago, they had sex. She licked his neck. She folded him to her as she always did, and she knew, even at that moment, she knew that when he came back to the room after his run, she would be gone.

How long had she been planning it? How many times had she opened herself to him, when she had no love for him, because she didn't want him to know she was about to leave?

He rang her again, and this time he waited for the message to end and he said, in a low voice that wouldn't carry through the bedroom wall, 'I wouldn't follow you if you begged me, you mad tart. Don't flatter yourself. I'm staying 'til Saturday. Make sure you're not in when I get back, Becks, or you'll wish you fucking weren't.'

His breath was jerky and he lay down on the unmade bed.

Would she ever hear it?

Becks. The planner.

By now her mobile might be in a recycling bin somewhere. New phone. New sim card. All the contacts neatly transferred. Except for him.

As he pictured her preparations, ran them through his mind, his body tensed. He played the movie in his head. Her pleasure at the process.

How many times had they sat at the kitchen table, making plans? Him with a bottle of chilled beer. Becks with a notepad and pen. Lists and flowcharts. He liked that in her. Her efficiency. Her organization. It took the burden off him. They usually ended up giving up half way and having sex. Then he'd put the television on, have another beer, and leave her to finish the plans. She'd get it all done, look over at him, smile and say, 'Sorted'.

Not this time.

He couldn't stay lying down.

Not now.

He sprang from the bed, jarring his heel as he landed awkwardly. Fuelled by the ever-renewable energy of anger. He picked up the camera bag, started to unzip it and then threw it back on to the bed.

Becks. The planner.

He could plan as well.

He stripped off, dipping his head to sniff the sweat of his armpits. Naked, he took the 'Do Not Disturb' sign and opened the door to hook it on the handle, half-hoping someone would pass and see him. The corridor was empty. He waited, aware that the small risk was arousing him. After a small hesitation he took back the sign and closed the door. Maybe someone would walk in.

By the time he reached the bathroom and twisted the shower control, he was fully aroused, anger, hate and excitement conjoining to drive him on. He kept the water as hot as he could bear it until he was discharged of desire. Then, after washing in warm water, he stood for fully three minutes under a cold drenching.

Belted into his towelling gown, he sat at the table in the window, fired up his laptop and turned his attention at last to the camera bag.

As he opened the flap, sand scattered on to the table top.

The bag had been resting against a clump of hardy grass in the sand dunes.

Ben hadn't even broken step. He spotted it from a distance on his run, scanned the area for signs of someone who might lay claim to it. Seeing no one he angled his path in its direction, dipped, caught hold of the strap and swung it over his shoulder, running on, and looking straight ahead.

If anyone stopped, him, well, he was doing a good turn, wasn't he? Rescuing it. Going to hand it in on his return to the hotel. No one saw him. No one stopped him. It was his now. Sorted.

Nice camera. Canon. He would have preferred Pentax, but there you go.

Ben ignored the extra lens and filters. Time enough to look at those later.

The camera was charged up and pinged when he turned it on. He flicked it over and snapped open the door for the memory card. 64 Gig. This guy was serious about his pictures. Pity he lost them.

He slid the card into the slot on the laptop.

Through the window, the beach and the sea. Everyone talked about the seals, but he'd never seen any. Just the usual hardy families, prepared to put up with the cold, Welsh sea. Once, he would have thought they were too poor to go to Spain or Turkey for the sun and warm water. Now, he knew that they were too rich, too middle-class to do that. They'd go skiing in the winter, maybe leave the kids at home for a week and go to Vienna or New York in the spring. But summer meant nostalgia on a British beach.

That was why they were here. Becks had come with her parents, and wanted to show it to him.

'Oh, please, Ben. Please. Can we? I'd love to show you the things I did when I was little.' She snuggled up to him. 'There's an old farmhouse. Totally deserted. When I was in the sixth form I used to fantazise about going there, with someone special, just the two of us.' She put her tongue into his ear. 'You know?'

He snapped open the folder on the desktop.

Hundreds of pictures spilled out. Small icons.

He clicked to 'slideshow' and waited for the scrolling to start.

Fucking seals. He could have guessed it.

Despite himself, Ben was impressed with the technique. Sun and waves, and sky and the groupings. These weren't just snapshots. They were good.

Ben leaned back, let his towelling robe fall open and looked out of the window again, keeping the slideshow in the corner of his eye.

He hit the pause button and logged on.

Find a price for the camera on Ebay.

While it was loading he clicked on his own pictures and pulled up the 'Becks' folder.

'The fuck?' he asked.

There was one picture. All the others had been trashed.

He clicked. The photo opened.

Becks. In their bedroom at home. Grinning at the camera, the middle finger of her left hand raised for him.

Planned.

Every move.

Long before they even came away.

The pictures were there yesterday. She must have wiped them while he was out running and put that one into the folder for him.

She was dead. She was so dead.

He grabbed his phone and hit her number.

Voice mail.

'I've changed my mind,' he said. 'Be there when I get back. Be there. And if you're not there, I'll find you. I know where to look. I'm going to fucking kill you.'

He highlighted his 'favourites' and clicked for www.rockyourgf.com.

He reckoned it was fifty-fifty fakes to real, at best. But the real ones were what he liked. People you might meet in the street. People like you. People like Becks. Actually, Becks herself.

He scrolled through the recent postings to where her pictures were.

'Removed at the Request of the Copyright Holder'

Scrolled back another couple of days.

'Removed at the Request of the Copyright Holder'

All of them. All gone.

She knew.

She'd found them.

He slammed down the lid of the laptop and stood up.

Walk.

Clear his mind.

He needed a plan of his own.

The seafront was quiet. Mainly old people. Half-term was last week, so the few families on the beach, enjoying the late autumn sun, were bunking off. Prepared to pay the fine.

So? Becks had found out about the website.

So what?

It was only a bit of fun. No harm done.

She should be proud of it.

Even Ben knew that this was stupid.

He hunched his shoulders, half in protection against the slight chill, half in anxious shame about what he'd done.

There was no harm in it, was there?

She'd let him take the pictures in the first place.

Most of them.

Some of them.

It was only when he sat down with his espresso and thought about his next move that he remembered the car.

He was stranded here. It would cost him a fortune to get home. How? Taxi to somewhere with a bus service. Bus to a station. Where would that be? Who the fuck took buses and trains these days?

Maybe there was a car hire place here?

By the time he left the coffee shop he had the name of a car hire firm just ten miles away, and the number for a taxi. He could drop the car off in London for ten percent extra. He'd sort it when he got to the place. They had lots of cars ready.

Just in case, though with no hope of success, he took a detour to the car park.

There it was.

Always the planner. Becks.

It was about the only thing that was his. Or it would be when he'd paid for it. The flat was in her name. Most of their stuff was hers. And so was over seventy percent of their joint income.

But the car was his, and she hadn't taken it to get home. She hadn't put a foot wrong. She hadn't even keyed it or trashed the lights.

Careful Becks.

Back in the room he rang Simon.

'Hey. Yeah, good. Well, no, not good, but anyway.'

'Yeah. I'll tell you. The thing is, can I crash at yours for a couple of days?'

'No. Well, yeah. Yeah, it's gone tits up. Yeah. All right. Thanks. I'll be there tonight.'

He closed the call and tried Becks again.

Voicemail. At least she hadn't closed the account. So she might pick this up.

'Look, Becks. I'm sorry. Ok? If you want to think again, we can. I can put it right. But I'll sleep at Simon's tonight. I'll get my things tomorrow. When you're at work. Give me a ring, ok? Sorry.'

It wouldn't work, but at least it might get him into the flat. Get his things. Then he could sort her out.

He threw his case on to the bed and grabbed things off the hangers.

The laptop was still on the desk. Might as well close it down properly.

He flipped the lid and punched in his password.

The slideshow was still running.

But no seals now.

It was Becks.

Someone had taken pictures of Becks, and they were on this camera?

Ben sat down. His breath was coming fast. The fist inside his stomach felt like anger, but he wasn't sure that it might not be fear. The overlap was too great.

Becks on her knees, looking over her shoulder.

Becks on her back, open, smiling.

Becks in boots. Just boots.

Becks with her mouth full, looking up at the camera lens.

And more. Becks doing things she had refused to do with him. And always, her partner, face out of shot, anonymous.

Ben found himself scrutinizing the body parts that he could see, nerving himself to ignore what the act was, trying to see if it was one partner or more. Two, several, lots?

The door opened and the chamber maid walked in. She looked at the pictures on the screen, grinned. Bitch.

'Sorry.'

Ben flipped down the lid of the laptop.

'Sorry,' she said again. But she didn't look it. She was the pretty one he had had hoped might walk in on him after his shower. But not hunched in front of a picture of a naked woman with, well, never mind.

'I thought the room was empty,' she said. She didn't back out, still grinned at him. Ben couldn't decide whether he wanted to punch her in the face or throw her on the bed. Either way, he wanted to wipe the grin off her face.

'Get out,' he said.

She turned to leave, then, at the last moment, she said, 'You just put the Do Not Disturb on the door, see? If you want to be private, like.'

She was gone before he could react.

Not wanting to be shamed into hanging the sign outside, he locked the door and fastened the chain.

He stood, looking out to sea. This was a lot to take in.

Becks, the planner.

The camera had been left for him.

Why not upload straight on to the laptop? Why take the risk?

Then the penny dropped.

This wasn't the point of the plan. He wasn't at the end of it. He was in the middle.

It was still being played out.

If he scrapped the memory card now, dumped the camera back on the sand dunes and drove away, he would be out of it. Plan over.

He knew he couldn't do it. He couldn't walk away. And Becks knew it, too.

Plan and Counter-plan.

He needed to know everything she'd done so far. It couldn't get any worse.

It got lots worse.

She knew everything. And it was all in the memory cards

There were more, in the pockets of the camera bag.

All right, he'd been a naughty boy. But, fuck, look at the pictures of Becks, getting shagged seven ways to breakfast time. She wasn't in the clear on this, was she?

The second card was Ben and Amy. Ben and Libby. Ben and that girl whose name he could never remember, the one he met in the bar after work.

Becks knew everything. She'd found his flash drives, sucked everything from them and put it on these cards.

So what? Come to think of it, he was glad she had. Fuck her. Fuck her, very much, thank you.

Ben grinned. At least she knew she wasn't the only one.

Who was he kidding? He stood up and paced the room. He'd rather have Becks back, not knowing, than no Becks because she'd found out.

All the same, it was good to look at the pictures again. That girl from the bar had been amazing. He scrolled through the slideshow to the end, and, seeing the final image, began to sweat.

It was a screen shot.

Him and Libby. www.cheatingbasturds.com/basturdben.

He clicked the link. And there he was. With all of them. She hadn't even fuzzed out his face. Anyone could see them. He clicked on a 'Report' button by the image.

'Image Locked'.

He grabbed his phone and jabbed her number.

'This isn't fucking funny, you bitch. Get that site cleared. You hear me? Get the fucking site cleared of my photographs. You hear me?'

Sweating, shaking, he threw it on the bed.

He forced himself to trawl through every image.

Oh, fuck, no. At work. In the office. With Amy. On his desk. On the floor. On Tony's desk. In Tony's oh-so-private office. He remembered it. Bank holiday.

'I've got to go in, Becks. Everything's gone to pieces. Audit next week. We're all expected to be there. Sorry. I'll make it up to you.'

It took Ben a while to realize that there was no one else posted on the site. It was his personal one. She'd created it, just for him. No one else could submit, and he couldn't remove anything. It was a fake. But it was a public fake. Anyone searching for revenge porn could find it.

This was way over the top. People cheat. Normal people deal with it.

Becks wasn't normal. This was mad.

He needed a plan.

First. Get the site taken down. Simon could sort that. Simon had contacts. But he'd have to put up with Simon's jibes forever. And what guarantee did he have that whoever took it down wouldn't keep the images? He would.

Double First. Get the site taken down, straight away. Before any twat on the internet copied the images and reposted them.

Ben groaned. That door must have shut ages ago. Once an image is up there it's there forever. Already he was on porn sites from Shanghai to the Galapagos Islands. Forever.

Second. Sort it out with work. There was no way they were not going to find out.

Fuck. Did that mad bitch know what she'd done? He was going to be sacked. Laughed at. People in bars would wonder where they knew his face from.

There were dozens of these images.

It took time for him to think that he was in just the same place that Becks was in as soon as he posted the first one of her.

Fuck that.

This was different. This was him.

He picked up his phone, and, without calling her number, spoke into the dead screen.

'I'm going to find you, Becks. I'm going to find you, and I'm going to hurt you. I'm going to hurt you a lot. More than you can imagine. You'll be fucking lucky if I don't kill you. Understand?'

He had to get back. He had to get to Simon's, fix up somewhere to live. Get the sites dealt with.

If he contacted Tony before he went back to work next week. Made a joke of it? Was there any need for that? Wait till he was found out? If he ever was?

Becks would know what to do. Becks always did.

He checked his emails before he finished up and checked out.

There was one from Becks.

Of course there fucking was. Of course.

Hi Ben,

I guess you know what's happening now. If you don't, stop reading this and check the camera bag. Neil saw you pick it up. Yes, he was watching. He's good at not being seen. And he's an absolute wizard with the internet, but you probably know that already.

Thanks for going to the old farmhouse with me. As you know, I always wanted to have sex there. But, and I really hope this doesn't upset you too much, you weren't the first. No. I know, it's disappointing, isn't it? But I had sex that last summer of school. There was a man at the hotel. A little bit older than me. And there was Neil as well. A couple of months ago when we set this up. You had that weekend training course? Remember? Except work doesn't pay for that sort of training, does it? The images are on your special site. I hope you've seen them. There have been others as well, over the years. In the farmhouse. It's been a very special place for me. But you were the last. I hope you appreciate that. I'm never going there again. But I've left some memories for the next people.

I would say it's been a pleasure, but, you know, it hasn't, really. I was quite glad when I found your little stash of memories. And when Neil hacked your laptop (yes, he's very clever with these things), and he found what you'd done to me, well, just say that the last couple of weeks have been a bit of a trial. The only consolation has been that every time you thought you were fucking me, I knew that I was really, really fucking you. Fucking you up. For good.

I had to take you to the ruined cottage, as a way of closing things for me. Everything started there, and a chapter of my life has ended. Neil made some nice presents for you and left them there. There are over hundred flash drives of the images of you. All over the cottage. In nooks and crannies. High up and low down. People will stumble over them for years to come. Even if you manage to take down the sites, they will always pop up again. But, I like to play fair. And here's a promise. I won't put them out anywhere else. And, there are more. Ones not on the internet, yet.

I've had the locks changed on the flat. All your things are packed up and I've sent them by courier to Simon's. That's where you'll go, isn't it? Anyway, if you go somewhere else, Simon will have your stuff.

Try one thing, just one, to get back at me and you'll really regret it. Neil has more things on you than you know even exist.

Becks.

PS. Tony at work already has the link to the website, so Monday morning should be interesting.

PPS. Here's a little something that Neil wanted to do. It's not free on the internet – yet. But if you try anything, it will be. The password is, Gideonosbourne11. The site is www.88timesacheater.com. Those images or flash drives at the farmhouse, too. Happy hunting.

He clicked the link, keyed in the password.

It was a fake. But a brilliant fake. Photoshop perfection.

Ben stared at himself giving a Nazi salute, wearing the uniform, having sex. Violent sex. He winced at the bloody, abused bodies, at his smug smile as he administered the cane, the lash. Him in some sleazy private room in a pub, with his mates (never seen before), Nazi posters and regalia.

The final image. The one she'd saved for best and last, was the interior of the farmhouse, plastered with posters of the worst of the pictures of him.

He packed his bag. Even with the driving urgency to get to the farmhouse, destroy the posters and the flash drives, he didn't throw his things into the case. He folded and arranged, keeping things neat and tidy.

It was a habit, too ingrained to resist, and it gave him time to think.

Damage-limitation, first.

Revenge, second.

By the time he snapped the lock on his case he had the first step settled in his mind.

The satnav had the farmhouse coordinates in its memory, so that was easy. Checkout was expensive. They charged him a full day he wasn't using, because he hadn't given notice of leaving early. He could live with that.

Damage-limitation. Revenge. That was all that mattered.

He stopped the car at the first petrol station, filled up and bought a petrol can.

'Friend's run out. I'm sorting it', he said, rolling his eyes. 'Women, eh? Have to do everything for them.'

Three more petrol stations. Three more cans. Three more gallons. By the time he got to the farmhouse he was well set.

He couldn't look at the pictures sprawled everywhere. He didn't even bother to look for the flash drives. They might be there. They might not. That was Becks all over. Get him searching for fuck all.

Didn't matter, anyway.

He had finished pouring the first can of petrol over the back wall when the voice startled him.

'What are you doing?'

Ben hadn't expected this. He thought he'd get a clear run.

'That's bloody dangerous,' said the man. He leaned in the doorway, and surveyed the scene. 'Those are you,' he said, nodding at the pictures.

'It's a joke,' said Ben. 'Stag night trick. Photoshop job. It's not me, really.'

The man wandered in. He was about the same height as Ben, but looked more solid, tougher. Ben didn't think he could take him on, so it had to be verbal.

'You know if your phone rings it will set this lot up with us in here, don't you?' the man said. 'Fumes.'

'It's in the car,' said Ben.

'Okay. Mine, too. He looked over his shoulder and called out, 'His phone's in the car.'

'What's up?' said Ben. 'What's going on?' He heard a car door slam, then Becks' voice.

'Got it.'

'What's going on?' he repeated.

'This is so much better,' said Becks, as she appeared in the doorway with his phone. 'Look. I'm getting a text.' Her own phone clanged and she read the text.

"Can't live with the shame. Can't live without you'. Oh, bless,' she said.

'Give me that.' Ben walked towards her, and the man punched him in the stomach. So hard that Ben fell on to his back.

'No bruises, mind,' said Becks.

"Going to end it all",' Becks read from her screen. 'Oh, Ben. You've made it so much easier. We had a plan, didn't we, Neil?'

'That's right,' said the man. 'We had a plan.'

'But it was messy, wasn't it?' she added. 'And risky.'

'Risky,' said Neil.

'We've got a rope,' she went on. 'You were going to hang yourself.'

Ben tried to get up and Neil kicked him back down. Choosing his spot for the kick to land.

'But if you'd struggled Neil would have had to hit you and we didn't want to leave any marks, so the petrol is much better.'

'Much better,' Neil agreed.

Becks leaned into Neil and licked his ear. 'Why didn't you think of petrol?' she asked.

He turned his head and kissed her, their open mouths hungry for each other.

'Anyway,' said Becks. 'Petrol it is.'

'You pour,' said Neil, 'I'll watch him.'

Ben tried over and over again to get to his feet. Neil was too strong, too fast.

'Actually,' said Becks, pouring the final can of petrol, 'you can bruise him as much as you like as long as you don't break any bones. There won't be any flesh left, will there?' She blew Ben a kiss. 'You are a sweetie, buying all this. And you paid by card, didn't you? Of course you did. So there's a lovely money-trail and it only leads to you.'

'Please don't. Please, Becks. I'm sorry. So sorry. Please. Don't burn me.'

'He's crying,' she said. The playfulness fell from her. 'Do you know how I cried? When I saw what you'd done? Pictures of me. On the internet like that. For ever. For fucking ever!'

'I'm sorry,' he said. 'Please.'

'Oh, shut him up,' she said. Neil kicked him hard in the stomach again, and he doubled up and retched.

'Off we go,' she said.

She struck a match and watched it flare up, then used it to light the other matches in the tray. Once they were burning well she tossed it through the window.

'Here goes,' she said.

The petrol ignited with a 'whoomph' which made her stagger back.

'I've lost my fucking eyebrows', she said.

Neil put his arms around her, lifted her up and swung her round and round, laughing.

She buried her face in his neck and laughed along with him.

Putting her down, they stood, side by side, hand in hand, watching the farmhouse burn.

'We'd better get away', she said. 'The smoke will attract people. 'But drive slowly.'

'Okay,' he agreed. 'Happy now? Is it sorted?'

She kissed him.

'Sorted.'

THROUGH THE MIST

MARTIN EDWARDS

Piper saw the farmhouse first. She was fifteen yards ahead of Jared, and long, impatient strides took her to the crest of the hill and a view of the narrow valley beyond. Limping in her wake, he was more bothered about his ricked ankle than having his breath taken away by the scenery. Panting with the effort, he joined her at the top. Piper stood motionless, her lips slightly parted.

The farm buildings squatted in a dip at the bottom of the slope. A dingy sign was nailed to the house, its faded lettering impossible to read. The windows were as dark as sightless eyes. No smoke rose from the chimneys, and Jared saw no cattle or goats or sheep. The barn was separated from the house by a yard in which young trees sprouted, their naked branches reaching up to the heavens as if pleading for mercy.

Mist oozed down the slopes on the far side of the valley. The sky, the bare land, and the damp haze were impossible to tell apart. Jared wanted to make a sour joke about fifty shades of grey, but Piper's rapt expression made him bite his tongue. She bent her head, as if in prayer. A minute passed.

'I'd better get back,' he said. 'Put some ice on this ankle. I think I've sprained it.'

Her silence resembled a shrug of indifference. It was as well he didn't expect sympathy. Stumbling over rain-greased rocks had done the damage. He was out of condition. Too many client lunches, dinners, and cocktail parties. Piper's gym membership cost a fortune, as did her personal trainer, but the investment of money and sweat was paying off. To watch her striding across the barren moorland, kitted for all weathers, you'd believe she was a country girl, born and bred.

He turned to go. 'Coming?'

'I want to look at that place.'

'It's a shell. Whoever lived there abandoned it long ago.'

She moved forward, intent on her quest. He grunted in reproach, but quietly enough for her not to hear. Retracing his steps, this time he took infinite care over the rocks, and made it back to Log Cabin without coming to further harm.

Two weeks of getting back to nature in a remote corner of Wales. Log Cabin had no electricity, no hot running water, and no refrigerator. Wi-fi was out of the question, and there wasn't a hope of a signal good enough to use a mobile. Water came from a spring by way of an outdoor tap; for bathing and everything else, there was a stream and a willow-fringed earth closet. An old cast-iron wood burning stove and a two-ring gas burner dominated the tiny kitchen. Illumination was supplied by lanterns, candles and torches. Outside, where the rutted track petered out and they'd parked their 4x4, was a small patio, where guests could warm themselves by a fire pit, provided it wasn't pouring down.

The holiday had seemed a good idea at the time. Piper had lost her job as editor of a glossy monthly magazine, and although she'd received a handsome pay-off in return for signing a gagging clause, her pride had suffered a mortal blow. She'd soared to the top of her profession, driven by a combination of ambition and barely suppressed rage in the relentless cycle of networking and back-biting that passed for celebrity journalism. But now circulation was plummeting, and the editor who had spent so many years living by the sword finally died by the sword.

She needed to escape from London, and the glamorous social world in which she'd become a non-person overnight. Jared was up for it. Over the past few years, the 24/7 world of graphic design had taken its toll. When he confided in his assistant that he felt burned out, Marissa soothed him with loyal reassurance, but he reasoned that if he took a break, she'd have a chance to prove her worth.

The Maldives would be nice, or perhaps Vietnam. But after a few minutes' web surfing, Piper fell in love with the notion of a fortnight in the wild and remote Preseli Mountains, and immediately began reinventing herself as a doughty environmentalist. International air travel was problematic, but guests at Log Cabin left only the lightest of footprints.

A nip of brandy revived his spirits, and half an hour with a cold compress against his ankle persuaded him that he'd only suffered a minor strain. Not enough to prevent him from walking over to the pub tonight. He deserved a treat.

Log Cabin wasn't so bad. It was owned by a gay couple who lived in Thatched Cottage at the top of the track. They had relocated to escape the hurly-burly of Newport, they'd explained, while pointing out the cabin's environmentally friendly features. Eco-paint inside and out, sheep's wool for insulation, and fair-trade organic cotton bed linen. Last night, after the long drive from Wimbledon, Jared and Piper had slept like Welsh lambs.

Piper did not arrive back until the light of day was fading, but she was uncharacteristically silent as she pulled off her new boots. When he asked if she was all right, she didn't reply.

He tried again. 'You didn't go inside that farmhouse?'

'The door wasn't locked. One of the window panes is missing. Of course I went in.'

'Go on, then... what's it like?'

He couldn't decode her expression. 'Nobody's lived there for years. Yet the house is full of old furniture, and things like china and cutlery. As if the people who lived there went out one day, and might come back at any moment.'

'Strange.'

'It's a special place. I've never known anything like it.'

'How do you mean?'

'It feels like... home.'

'A derelict farmhouse in the middle of nowhere? How can that feel like home?'

She snorted. 'No use trying to explain to someone like you.'

'Someone like me? Come on, I'm all ears.'

But he had annoyed her, and she refused to say anything else, insisting she was worn out after her exertions. After a bite to eat, she announced she was going straight up to bed. He didn't feel tired, and when he said he might stroll down to the pub for a quick one, she didn't argue. Nor did she ask after his injured ankle.

The Bluestone, a thirty minute walk from the cabin, took its name from the dark, heavy rocks found here. Bluestones from the Preseli Mountains had supposedly been used to build much of Stonehenge, but nobody knew how prehistoric men had transported them to a site in Wiltshire, two hundred and fifty miles away.

As Jared stepped through the door, he was conscious of chatter coming to a sudden halt, and felt the locals' eyes locking on to him. The pub smelled damp and felt draughty, and made few concessions to customer care. No music, no weekly quiz, no flat screen television to entertain football fans. Even the fire in the tiny inglenook was dying. The decor looked ancient, and so did the cadaverous landlord.

Jared tried to strike up a conversation as the landlord filled his tankard, but friendliness was rewarded with grudging monosyllables. The man only managed a full sentence when Jared asked about the abandoned farmhouse in the valley.

'Evans Farm? You don't want to go messing about there.'

'What do you know about the place?' It wasn't the response Jared had hoped for. 'It seems uninhabited, but my wife says it's still full of furniture.'

Actually, he and Piper were not husband and wife, but they'd been living together longer than plenty of married couples managed. Five years, or was it six?

The landlord's watery eyes blinked. 'She's not been inside?'

'Out of curiosity, yes.'

'Make sure she doesn't go there again.'

'I'm sorry. Honestly, she didn't mean to trespass or do any damage.'

'It's not safe.'

'How do you mean?'

The landlord showed yellow teeth in a dreadful smile. 'Some folk call it Hell Farm.'

A wizened old fellow wearing an eye patch said something in Welsh, and the landlord shuffled over to serve him. Their conversation was unintelligible to Jared, and he pulled a chair up to the inglenook. The fire was reduced to its last embers. The men glanced in his direction several times, and he knew they were talking about him. He drained his glass, and headed back to the cabin. When he climbed under the duvet (organic merino wool, the owners said proudly), Piper was snoring.

He woke to the relentless clatter of rain against the wooden roof. Piper was already up and dressed. As he slotted two slices of wholegrain into the toaster, he repeated what the landlord had said.

'You should never have opened your mouth!'

'I was only making polite...'

'People in the village don't have a clue. It's nobody else's business what I do here.'

'Okay, okay, but I thought I'd better pass on his warning. The building's obviously unsafe. I'm surprised people are able to get inside. There may be rotten floorboards, all sorts of hazards.'

'I'm going back to the farm this morning.'

The toaster pinged. 'What on earth for? You've poked around already.'

'If I tried to explain, you wouldn't understand'

'You're dead right. I don't understand.'

'The story of your life,' she muttered.

She stomped out of the cabin without another word. Deterred by the rain, Jared stayed inside for most of the day, glancing at a local guidebook before settling down with an Oxford paperback edition of The Mabinogion. He ventured outside only when the downpour eased to a dreary drizzle in early afternoon.

Heading east, he followed a byway that took him towards a burial cairn on the brow of a small hill. This area was as rich in Neolithic remains as in Celtic legends. A buzzard hovering above the old pile of stones gave a plaintive cry. Long before Jared reached the cairn, it vanished from sight.

Through a faint mist, he saw a dozen wild ponies, black, brown, and white, roaming across the grassland, the wind ruffling their manes. He yanked his new binoculars out of their case, but by the time he'd fiddled with the focusing wheel, the ponies were lost in a shroud of grey. The rain was teeming down again, and he was ready to call it a day.

Piper arrived at the cabin after he did. Her hair was damp, and her wrinkles more obvious than ever. At moments like this, he remembered he was seven years her junior. When they'd met, she'd made all the running. Their first date had been her idea. He'd soon found himself swept away. She liked to describe herself as an irresistible force.

'Where did you get to?' he asked.

'The farmhouse.'

'Where else?'

'Nowhere else. I feel I belong there.'

'How do you mean?'

Her expression of distaste suggested that his puzzlement amounted to a lack of empathy verging on betrayal. For such a strong woman, Jared thought, she was surprisingly needy. More than once over the years, she'd made him jump through hoops of her own devising to prove his devotion. Marissa, in whom he'd confided, said it was because of the age gap. She diagnosed Piper as insecure.

'Already I think of it almost as home.'

Time to lighten the mood. 'Put in an offer, then! At least you can be sure of getting vacant possession. I bet it's going dirt cheap. Bring in contractors to do it up, then spend a fortnight a year there, and rent it out the rest of the time. Might even be a good investment.'

She shook her head. A blank look glazed her eyes. When Piper was in this sort of mood, there was no reasoning with her. Changing tack, he told her of an old story he'd read in the book of legends, about a doomed quest to find true love, but she yawned loudly, and he gave up. Soon she took herself off to bed again, and he decided to risk a return visit to The Bluestone.

As he walked through the door, he spotted the couple who owned the cabin sitting near the open fire. They invited him to join them, and he bought a round of drinks.

'Your good lady not with you?' This was from Robert, bespectacled, prim, and at least ten years older than his partner.

'No, Piper's having an early night.'

'Done a lot of walking, have you?'

'She was out most of the day.' Jared swallowed a mouthful of beer. 'There's a place she finds fascinating. We came across it yesterday. Evans Farm, I think it's called.'

Robert exchanged a glance with David, a young man with a mass of dark, curly hair. Both men were actors, but times were hard in their line of business, they said. At present, both of them were resting. The proceeds of the sale of Robert's late parents' house in Notting Hill had paid for their cottage, as well as the construction of the log cabin. The rental income kept them ticking over while they waited for their agent to find them a decent script.

'Nobody's lived there for years,' Robert said. 'It's all shut up.'

'The door isn't locked, apparently. She was able to walk straight in.'

Robert frowned. 'I wouldn't advise that. Risky, you know.'

'Risky?'

'It's in a rotten state of repair. There's an open well in the yard, you know.'

'I suppose it could be done up. Modernised.'

'It'll never happen,' Robert said.

'I suspect Piper has got some wild idea into her head.' Jared gave a scornful little laugh, to emphasise the wildness of it. 'She'd rather like to own the place.'

'Oh no. It's not for anyone else to possess.'

'Not for sale? Surely whoever owns it would be glad if someone took it off their hands. It's not doing anyone any good at present.'

'There are complications,' David said quickly. 'Uncertainty about who owns the building. So I've heard. The people who lived there had no children, no close family. Your wife should look elsewhere. Rosebush, say, or Maenclochog.'

Robert gave an imperceptible nod as his partner spoke. Lacking the energy to pursue the matter, Jared asked if there was hope of better weather tomorrow, and was duly reassured. The three of them finished their drinks and left together. When they reached the gate of Thatched Cottage, and Jared said goodbye, Robert leaned towards him, and hissed in his ear.

'Remember, they call that place Hell Farm for a reason. I know what I'm talking about. Make sure your wife realises, it's not a place for her.'

'I'll do my best.' Jared strove for a jocular tone. 'But she's a strong-willed woman.'

'Nobody is strong all the time.' Robert laid a hand on Jared's arm. 'Go safely.'

Jared splashed through the mud back to Log Cabin. He wasn't ready for bed, and started poring over The Mabinogion. When his eyelids began to droop, he undressed, and climbed under the duvet. Piper's snoring was louder than he could ever remember.

Next morning he tried to tell her about his chat with Robert and David, but she didn't want to discuss Evans Farm, and brushed aside his suggestion that, since the rain had relented, they might walk out in the direction of some Neolithic remains on the other side of the hamlet.

'You do that if you like,' she said. 'It's not for me.'

For a moment, he contemplated challenging her about the nonsense of obsessing over an old farmhouse going to rack and ruin. But he contented himself with a non-committal grunt, and returned to Math fab Mathonwy, and the story of Blodeuwedd, the faithless woman of flowers.

Hateful Blodeuwedd had just been transformed into an owl when a loud rap on the door made Jared start. They'd not had a single visitor since their arrival. He supposed it must be Robert, come to reiterate his warning about Evans Farm.

Wrong again. He opened the door to find Marissa beaming at him. Clutched in her hand was a plastic wallet full of papers. She kissed him chastely on the cheek, and raised her eyebrows in a question. Piper, he explained, had gone out walking. He'd no idea when she'd be back.

'What brings you here?'

'Corluka is complaining about the re-brand. I'm worried he'll terminate our retainer. I thought I'd better bring the emails so you can decide what we should do. God, what a journey. I set off at the crack of dawn, and it's still taken forever to get here. I never knew places as cut-off as this still existed. Though it's lovely. If you like that sort of thing.'

He waved her inside, and scanned the documents while she exclaimed about the cosiness of the cabin. Corluka was a pain, but there was nothing here that Marissa couldn't have dealt with. She'd surrendered to curiosity, that was the truth of it. And, Jared realised, she wanted to see him just as much as he'd yearned to see her.

He put the printed emails back in the wallet, and told her he'd draft a response to the client. She kissed him again, a little less chastely this time, but he pushed her gently away.

'Piper could come back any minute.'

'Where is she?'

He told her about the abandoned farmhouse, and what he'd been told by the landlord, and by Robert and David. Her pixie face twisted into a parody of ghoulishness.

'Creepy!'

'We could go out for a walk ourselves.'

'To this place, Evans Farm?'

'No.' He didn't want to disturb Piper in – whatever she was doing. 'There's a circle of stones mentioned in the guidebook. Do you have walking boots?'

'In the car,' she said exuberantly. 'Bought them yesterday, along with this jacket. I don't need to dash back to the office. It's Saturday tomorrow. After coming all this way, I might as well take a look at darkest Pembrokeshire. I've booked into a B&B about three miles away.'

She'd planned it all out, Jared realised. That's what made her such an asset in the business, her clear thinking and attention to detail. He didn't care to think how Piper would react to her arrival. The pair had met several times, and hadn't bonded. Marissa was young, energetic, and brimming with enthusiasm, while Piper was, well, Piper. They had little or nothing in common. Except Jared.

He checked the map. If they dropped her bag at the B&B, they could leave her car there, and walk to the stone circle before returning over the moor to Log Cabin. For once, it wasn't raining, and only a few threads of mist clung to the rust-coloured slopes. He'd read that it was best to follow sheep tracks, to avoid the boggiest ground, and their route skirted a stretch of marshland, before they emerged from a beech coppice on to grassy heath coloured by gorse in flower and vivid splashes of purple heather. A red kite swooped on some unsuspecting prey in the distance, and wild ponies galloped on the horizon.

Marissa's blue eyes sparkled as he told her about the Mabinogion, and its tales of vengeful giants and cursed heroes, beautiful women and ancient enchantments. Perhaps someone had put a spell on the abandoned farmhouse; that might explain why Piper found it so fascinating.

'Guess how she'll describe it if she turns it into an upmarket guest house?' Jared smiled. When talking to Marissa, he always portrayed Piper as a PR obsessive. 'Soak yourself in the lore of Merlin, Arthur, and Old Magick...'

'Don't forget eco-sustainability.' Marissa gave a conspiratorial grin.

The fresh air and exercise helped to make up his mind. He wouldn't ruin the holiday, but once the fortnight was up, he'd tell Piper they needed a break from each other. If she wanted to buy the old farmhouse, fine. Let her bury herself down here if she wished. After two weeks, he'd be desperate for the bright lights and, yes, the congestion and the carbon. If you were tired of London, you were tired of life.

Piper returned to the cabin half an hour after them. She glared at Marissa, and paid no attention as Jared explained in detail why it had been so important for him to be consulted in person about how to handle the disgruntled client. Marissa was young enough to believe that no-one could remain immune to her charm forever, and after a few exclamations about the beauties of the landscape, she succumbed to the temptation to ask about Evans Farm.

'Jared tells me you've fallen in love with an old farmhouse. You might even put in an offer, and do it up?'

Piper's face darkened. 'There's absolutely no question of doing it up, as you put it.'

'But if nobody's lived there for years?'

'It would be sacrilege to make changes. You don't understand.' Piper's steady gaze took in Jared as well. 'Neither of you.'

'Fair enough.' Jared opted for bonhomie. 'Let's talk about dinner. What would you like, darling?'

'I'm not hungry.'

'Are you all right?'

'Never better,' she said softly. 'And now I'm going to bed. I need my rest.'

She walked out without sparing Marissa a glance. Jared caught the girl's eye, and gave a helpless shrug. Following Piper into the bedroom, he closed the door carefully, and said, 'What's the matter?'

Piper, perching on the edge of the bed, paused in the act of pulling off her socks. 'Why did you have to bring her here?'

'I didn't!' he insisted. 'This contract is one of our top revenue-earners. If Corluka decides...'

'I'm not a fool, Jared,' she said. 'You're flaunting your mistress in front of my eyes.'

'She's not my mistress!'

'You must think I was born yesterday.' Her lips formed into a curious smile. 'Well, I was born a long time ago.'

'What are you talking about?'

'She can't possess you, Jared.'

'You're not well, Piper. I think you're right, it's best for you to get some sleep.'

Closing the door behind him, he moved towards Marissa, and put a hand on her arm. 'Let's go.'

'Where?'

'The Bluestone? The menu isn't up to much. Pie and chips is as good as it gets.'

'We could go to the B&B, if you like,' she whispered.

'I'll take you back there later, of course.' He didn't want to seem too eager. Not yet. 'You don't want to have to walk all that way in the dark.'

'You'd better not have too much to drink.'

'Don't worry,' he said, pretending not to catch her drift. 'I'll drive slowly. All those bends in the road, you can't put your foot down.'

Ten minutes later, they were at the bar of The Bluestone, ordering pie and chips from the grizzled landlord. If the man considered it strange that Jared had a different female companion tonight, he kept his thoughts to himself. His main aim seemed to be to rebuff attempts at polite conversation.

'What a charmer,' Marissa said, when they'd settled at the table by the inglenook. 'Could he tell I wanted to ask him what was so special about Evans Farm?'

Jared sipped the foam off his pint. 'I don't... oh, hello, there!'

David had walked in through the front door. He waved in greeting, and after he'd bought himself a glass of wine, he came over, and Jared invited him to pull up a chair. After introducing Marissa, he explained that Piper was weary, and didn't feel up to a night out.

'Did she go out today?'

Jared nodded. 'Back to that old farmhouse.'

'You're not serious?' His voice was hushed. 'After what Robert told you both?'

'He didn't tell us much, to be fair, did he? Once Piper's mind is made up, she won't allow herself to be deflected. She's really taken a shine to the place, God knows why. You'd almost think it has a hold over her.'

'You mustn't let her go there again. It's dangerous.'

'Why?' Marissa leaned across the table. 'Why is it dangerous?'

David looked over his shoulder. The landlord was deep in conversation with the old man who wore the eye patch. Their pies and chips didn't appear to be imminent.

'It's not a story that people want to talk about. They reckon it's bad luck.'

Jared clicked his tongue. 'Old-fashioned superstitions won't cut any ice with Piper. I'm surprised you and Robert go along with them.'

'All right. I'll tell you.'David cleared his throat. 'This is between you and me, mind. Not a word to Robert, or...'

'He'll kill you?' Marissa smiled.

Jared squeezed her hand, hard enough to make her flinch. 'Please, go on.'

'Evans Farm was owned by Euros Evans. His family farmed on the hills for generations, but he was the last of the line. A cussed, bad-temped old bachelor. He ill-treated his own animals, and he liked human beings even less. His livestock had dwindled to a handful of sheep and pigs, by the time he took a shine to a girl in the village. Her parents had died, and she scraped a living, taking in laundry. Thirty years separated them in age, but Euros was desperate for a son and heir. When they got married, the gossips reckoned she was already pregnant, but the baby was stillborn. Euros blamed her, and people would sometimes see her with bruised cheeks or sporting a black eye. Not that they often saw her. Euros believed a woman's place was in the home, and as the years went by, months could pass without her venturing as far as the village. Once he took her to hospital with a badly broken arm. An accident she said, but folk round here aren't fools. There was a young man called Lomax who delivered the post to the farm, and he took a shine to her. Euros warned him off, but

Lomax saw himself as a knight in shining armour. Determined to save the damsel in distress.'

David paused to sip at his drink. A line of sweat on his brow suggested that telling the story was a physical strain. 'One foggy day, in the depth of winter, the postman never completed his round. Nobody saw him again. The girl vanished at the same time. Euros insisted they'd run off together, but no trace of either of them was ever found.'

'What do you think happened?' Marissa breathed.

'I don't know. This was long before we moved here, but the rumour-mongers said he'd hit each of them over the head with his spade, before feeding them to his pigs.'

'Omigod!'

Panic flared in David's eyes, as he glanced round to see if anyone had heard. 'Quiet! Folk may gossip here, but they don't like to discuss these things with strangers. That's why...'

His voice faltered, and he lifted his glass hastily to his lips, spilling some of the beer as he did so.

'That's why what?' Jared asked.

'When Robert and I were looking round here, we found the cottage. It had potential, and we assumed it would be dirt cheap. Damp, of course, in the valley, but... anyway, he went for a look around one day, and when he came back to Newport, he seemed different, somehow. Changed.'

'In what way?'

'He was surly, and aggressive, almost as if calling at the farm had changed his attitude to our relationship.' David closed his eyes. 'I may as well admit, at that time, there was an old friend of mine he didn't care for. All perfectly innocent, but Robert got the wrong idea. He's always been... possessive. He threatened to leave me, if I didn't stop seeing Tim.'

'You can't believe this was connected to the farm?' Marissa said.

David bristled. 'You don't have to listen.'

'Please,' Jared said. 'Don't mind Marissa. Tell us about you and Robert.'

'He tried to find out if the farm was for sale, but the estate agencies were no help. They steered us towards Thatched Cottage, and I begged Robert to put in an offer. I offered to stop seeing Tim, and gradually Robert became his old self again. He never went back to Evans Farm. When I asked around, I pieced together the story of Nerys Evans, and young Lomax.'

'So Euros Evans got away with murder?'

'It did him no good. He stopped caring for himself, and drank heavily. One misty morning, the new postman heard a commotion in the piggery. Euros had fallen over in a stupor, and knocked himself out, or perhaps he'd had a heart attack. The animals were having a feast. He'd not fed them for days, it seemed.'

'I think I'm going to be sick,' Marissa said, and ran off to the toilet.

Jared said, 'So that's why people say Evans Farm is dangerous?'

'The danger is real. I'm sorry, but you need to give up your lady friend.'

'Marissa works for me,' Jared snapped. 'We have a purely professional relationship.'

'As you wish.' David drained his glass. 'You need to get away from Evans Farm. Go tomorrow. We'll refund your payment, if that bothers you.'

'Piper will never agree. She hates people telling her what to do.'

'This has never happened before to anyone who has rented the cabin. Something in her nature must be drawn to Evans Farm.'

'No, I think she sees a business opportunity.'

David stood up. 'I must go. Robert will be anxious. I just need to get away sometimes, have some space to myself.'

'Like Piper.'

Behind the bar, the landlord raised his hand. The food was ready. David strode out into the night, and Jared was pouring brown sauce over his pie by the time Marissa returned. Her cheeks were pale but her jaw was set.

'He just wanted to freak me out. People round here can't have anything better to do with their time than make up spooky stories. They'd be better sticking to the Mabinogion.'

He drove her to the B&B, but she didn't ask him in, and to his surprise, he felt relieved. They agreed that she'd come over to Log Cabin first thing, and he'd try to talk some sense into Piper. When he arrived back at the cabin, he could hear loud snoring the moment he unlocked the door. He glanced at Piper as he got into bed, and decided she was looking gaunt and old. Never before had her cheeks seemed so leathery, her brow so deeply creased.

A restless night was crowded with dreams of knights on horseback going into battle, tormented maidens seeking sanctuary, and old, foul-smelling hags spitting out imprecations. He awoke with a confused recollection of a thatched farmhouse, burning to the ground, but the sight had made him happy rather than sad, because some dreadful enemy was perishing in the flames.

Blinking, he realised that Piper was already dressed, and pulling on her boots.

'I need to tell you something,' he croaked.

'Come to the farm. We can talk there, for as long as you wish.'

'No. Last night, Marissa and I met David. He told us all about the farm.'

'I don't listen to tittle-tattle, and if you know what's good for you, neither will you. The girl's leading you astray. She doesn't belong here.'

'Neither do we.'

Piper paused in the act of tying her laces. 'You couldn't be more wrong.'

'The farm has a history.' His brain was scrambled; he couldn't find the words that would make her pay attention to what he had to say. 'It's not a happy story.'

She reached for her jacket. 'Join me there, as soon as you're up. You'll see why the farm means so much to me. It's not too late for us, we can make it work. We don't need anyone else. Just the two of us, again.'

A smile flitted across her face. She seemed excited, fizzing with energy, and for an instant he remembered what had first attracted him to her. But when she dropped a kiss on his cheek, her lips were as cold as snow.

Marissa arrived as he was finishing his breakfast, and when he explained that Piper had already set off for Evans Farm, she seized his hand.

'Come back to London. Terrible things have happened at that farm. David's right, she should have kept away.'

'I can't just up and go.'

'She's not behaving rationally. I think she's having a breakdown.'

'All the more reason not to desert her now.' He took a deep breath. 'I'll sort it out once and for all. I'm going to the farm, and I'll tell Piper that we need to pack our bags, and leave. She needs help. Treatment of some kind.'

'She'll take no notice. It's part of the illness.'

'I owe it to her to try. It's all right. You set off home.'

'I'm not leaving you here.'

'You can't come. Please, Marissa. She won't listen to me if you're there.'

'No, it's better that we both go. It's time for a few home truths. If you ask me, you're the one in danger, not Piper. I won't let you face it alone.'

He shook his head, but didn't answer. Folding her arms, she waited for him to get ready.

Outside, threads of mist blurred the trees. The air felt moist, and the breeze nipped at their exposed cheeks, but before long they were scrambling over the slippery surface of the rocky outcrop where he'd hurt his ankle last time.

'Five more minutes, and we'll be on the brow of the hill,' he gasped, 'You'll be able to look down at the farm for yourself.'

'Are you sure we will be able to see?' she asked, only half-joking. 'The mist is thickening.'

She hurried ahead of him, and he didn't catch up until he reached the ridge above the valley. They could see Evans Farm at the bottom of the dip, but the mist was encroaching on the outbuildings, and the rusty hill slopes were no longer visible. Above, the clouds were dark and threatening, with no hint of the brightness that might disperse the blanket of murk.

'I've never seen anywhere so bleak and miserable.' She shivered. 'Or so eerie. It's as if the whole place is sullen and brooding. After those terrible things happened.'

He nodded, said nothing.

'Do you think Piper is inside the house?'

'Where else can she be?'

'Perhaps it's more comfortable inside than it looks,' Marissa said. 'Though it's hard to believe. What should we do?'

He started down the slope. 'I need to look for her.'

'Be careful! She's unstable, Jared. Don't let her ruin your life too, she's not worth it!'

She watched for a few moments, then picked her way after him. The terrain wasn't difficult, even though the ground was bumpy, and slick with moisture. The Preseli Mountains were not very steep. They weren't really mountains at all.

Jared reached level ground, and pushed aside the old barred gate. He walked forward until he was facing the front door, when he came to a halt. Putting on a spurt, Marissa caught up with him.

'Danger.' She pointed to the notice on the wall. 'I guess it all contributes to the legend of Hell Farm, huh? Quiet enough now, but nobody in their right mind would want this as a holiday home. I suppose that's the real reason the place was left to rot.'

He gestured towards the building to their left. 'That must have been the piggery. Scene of the crime.'

'Don't! You'll make me feel queasy again. Thank God the pigs are long gone. What sort of a man could treat people like that?'

'He was evil,' Jared muttered. 'Decaying, putrid evil.'

She threw him a sharp glance. 'Are you okay?'

'I need to rescue her,' he said. 'Before it's too late.'

'The mist is closing in on us. Shit, why did I trek out to this God-forsaken spot?'

'You made a choice. I begged you not to come.' He took a breath. 'Now there's no way back.'

'What are you talking about?'

He pointed in the direction of the slope they had descended. It was cloaked in mist. Only the farm house was visible. The rest of the valley and the hills had vanished.

'We know the path back to the cabin, even if we can't see it.' Her voice faltered. 'We aren't completely lost. If we stick close to each other, everything will be all right.'

'You'll never manage it. Besides, I have to save Piper.'

'Saver her from what? She's the one who fell in love with this place. For all we know, she's curled up inside, smoking weed, and perfectly happy.'

'I need to find her.' He moved forward. "Wait here if you want.'

'No, you can't leave me alone out here!'

When he kept walking, she called, 'Wait!' and ran after him. They arrived at the front door at the same moment. There was no knocker, no bell push, but it didn't matter. The door was ajar.

'You go first,' she breathed.

As he shoved the door open, she glanced over her shoulder. The mist was everywhere. Visibility was ten feet, no more. She couldn't even see the barred gate. They might have been anywhere.

The interior was very dark. They entered a large hall. Doors on either side were firmly closed. Ahead was a wooden staircase, and beyond that a narrow passageway leading to the rear of the farmhouse. There must have been an open or broken window upstairs, since down the staircase floated tiny wisps of mist.

'What's that?' Marissa whispered in Jared's ear.

The treads of the staircase creaked. Someone was moving down the steps. There was a faint whiff of something stale.

'Jared? Is that you?'

It was Piper's voice, surely, and yet it wasn't Piper's voice. Hoarse and reedy, it sounded as if it belonged to someone old. An old man, rather than an old woman?

'Yes.' As he answered, Marissa slipped her hand into his. Both of them were trembling.

'Are you alone? Has she gone?'

Marissa gripped his fingers so tightly that he nearly cried out.

'Piper, this can't go on. I need to take you back to London.'

'This is my home,' the voice said. 'The farm belongs to me, and so do you. I ask you again. Is she gone?'

'I'm here!' Marissa cried out. 'Why are you doing this to him? It's so cruel. You're not well, I realise, but this is no place for any of us. He needs to get away.'

A faint moan came from the staircase. So much mist was gathering, that now they could only see the bottom step of the staircase. But the treads began creaking again under heavy footsteps, and slowly, slowly, a figure emerged out of the grey nothingness.

And yes, it was Piper, but it wasn't Piper. Twill shirt, grey trousers, hobnailed boots; those weren't her clothes. She moved to the lowest step, and her face became clear through the mist. Hollow eyes, broken nose, gapped teeth, these were not her features, or if they were, they had become distorted by time and trouble. Her slim, manicured hands had become withered claws. Piper had aged, more years than he dared to guess.

Marissa squealed as Piper advanced. Jared moved his body between them, forming a human shield. Piper stretched out her arms in front of her, and he caught hold of the claw-like hands. But he dropped them as quickly, letting out a shriek of pain, and fell to his knees. Marissa turned, and pulled open the door.

'Come on, run! She'll never be able to catch us, not – not like that.'

Piper bent over him, and he looked imploringly into the hollow eyes.

'What's happened here?' he whispered.

'This is where you and I belong,' Piper breathed. 'Everything we possess is in this house.'

Marissa shouted, 'Jared, we need to run! Don't let her touch you again!'

She stumbled outside. The mist was billowing like a cloud of steam. From the distance came a steady, rhythmic noise. Not thunder, surely? She looked left and right, but it was impossible to see anything. The ground beneath her feet was rocky and uneven. She turned around, unable to keep her bearings.

Jared hauled himself back to his feet. Piper stretched out her arms once more, and he lost his footing, yet somehow managed to evade her grasp, and drag himself towards the door.

Piper gave a throaty chuckle. 'You won't escape. She hasn't.'

Outside, a pounding sound, almost like the clatter of hooves, thudded through the mist. Marissa screamed, a short and piercing cry of terror, but she was invisible in the gloom. Jared blundered this way and that, disorientated and frightened. The mist clutched at his throat. It was as if he'd been blinded. He could no longer see Piper, and his head was spinning. The pounding of hooves grew louder. The din reached a crescendo as a baleful brown face reared out of the grey nothingness.

The feral ponies had come to Evans Farm.

Backing away, he collided with something. Another pony. He was surrounded.

'Jared!'

Piper sounded distraught, as if realising that the end was near. He staggered a couple of paces, and then was almost felled by a brutal blow to the back. A pony had kicked him. Somehow he kept his balance, but the animals were agitated, and he understood that they did not mean to let him go. Teeth sank into the shoulder of his jacket, and when he tried to shrug off the attack, a kick in the stomach doubled him up, and his feet gave way under him. But the ground was not there to break his fall. He seemed to drop several feet, before he caught hold of an iron bar.

He was inside the well. Above, the ponies were crowding round, the stamping their hooves making such a din that he could not think. The iron bar was slimy, and he felt his grip loosening. Something brushed his fingertips, something freezing cold and horrible.

Piper had found him, but it was too late for both of them.

He released the bar, and with a final effort of will, seized the offered claw, pulling her down, down, down, to accompany him into damp and dark oblivion.

HOUSE GUEST
HELENA EDWARDS

'Well, I'm enjoying myself, Ro, even if you aren't,' said Mum. 'I can't believe you'd rather be cooped up in London than out here, in this beautiful place...'

'What are you doing?'

The girl's voice took us both by surprise. We had been so absorbed in our bickering, we had not heard her approach. Through the door – left open to allow the smell of paint to escape – I could see the sun dropping behind the Welsh hills, lighting up the fair hair which hung like curtains on either side of her thin face. Her navy blue coat drooped from her shoulders, the sleeves covering her hands.

My mother recovered first.

'We're painting a Welsh dragon on this wall,' she said, gesturing with a brush which dripped vermilion paint. 'Do you like it?'

The girl shrugged her shoulders. 'Suppose so. What's wrong with wallpaper?'

No answer occurred to us. Instead, my mother held out her hand. 'I'm Martha McCullen and this is Rowena. Who are you?'

'Ceri from Ellis' farm, over there.' She nodded, in an easterly direction. 'I help my dad out, and I used to do odd jobs here too. I came to ask you, will you have any work going?'

'Well, we're not going to be doing any farming here. We just bought the house to live in.'

Ceri looked crestfallen, and Mum said, 'We might be able to offer you some other sorts of work. This house hasn't been lived in for a year since the Pughs left, and I'm planning to do a lot of entertaining, so it needs some work.'

'Entertaining? Like singing, you mean?'

'No.' Mum smiled. 'I mean dinner parties. We have a lot of friends in London who'll come at weekends, to get some peace and quiet in the countryside. You could help me in the kitchen. Do you know how to cook any traditional Welsh dishes?'

Ceri looked more puzzled than ever.

Mum handed her one of Dad's old shirts. 'Why don't you put this on and help us out with the mural, and then I'll see if I can find you some more work.'

Ceri took the brush and joined in, watching Mum carefully and imitating her. As she got into the swing of the painting, and prompted by Mum's questions, she became talkative. She and her dad had been alone since her mother left to live with a woman in Swansea, when Ceri was six. The children at her school said her dad had killed her mum and fed her body to the pigs, but it wasn't true. Ceri hadn't liked anyone at that school, they weren't very nice. She hadn't liked the Pughs either, the last people to live in our new house. Old Mr Pugh had shot her dog. He said it had been chasing sheep, but it wasn't true. He had died after falling off a ladder. Ceri thought the farm was haunted by his ghost.

Mum shuddered. 'What nonsense!'

At eighteen, Ceri was four years older than I was and had led a very different sort of life. But I too knew what it was to be an outsider at school. We had moved around, and I was used to being the new girl who never fitted in. I had learned that it was unusual to have parents who worked in the film industry, and that to talk of trips to America and parties with film stars led, if not to incredulity, to suspicion, envy and even dislike.

I had not been impressed when my parents bought a derelict farmhouse in the middle of nowhere. My first sight of it, at the end of a long, narrow lane, with tiles missing from the porch roof, had done nothing to reassure me. What, I demanded, was I supposed to do there?

Mum said I could invite a friend to stay, but I could think of no one who would accept my invitation. Green fields, mud, me and a load of sheep for company – who would go for that? We even had to put buckets under the holes in the roof when it rained.

So I was pleased when Ceri walked through our door that day, and even more pleased when she seemed impressed to learn about my father's job as a writer of screenplays. Chatting to her made the work of preparing the house for our first guests a lot more pleasurable than it would have been otherwise.

Our guests arrived for a housewarming party that weekend. They were a couple of artists who were also practising Buddhists and, by far my favourite, my godfather and Dad's oldest friend, Alistair. Although Mum dismissed the idea that Mr Pugh might be haunting our house, she decided not to take any chances. As the sun set, the Buddhists conducted a candlelit procession through each room and outbuilding, with chanting and incense. Distant rumbles of thunder contributed to the atmosphere. Dad and Alistair, already drunk, stumbled along in their wake, laughing together.

Later, while a vegetarian stew simmered in the Aga, filling the house with the smells of Moroccan spices, Alistair and Dad went out into the farmyard with two old shotguns they had discovered in the barn. They tested them on a series of targets, including empty wine bottles, sending shards of glass all over the yard. They came in when the rain started, Mum lit the candles in their silver sticks on the long wooden table, and ladled out the lentil stew.

Ceri arrived to wash up while we were eating. I saw her watching us from the kitchen doorway when she thought no one was looking, and munching on a sandwich. Alistair came over and whispered in

Mum's ear – I was sitting next to her so heard every word – 'Did you know that a vision of loveliness has materialised in your kitchen?'

'Ceri. Our neighbour's daughter, yes.'

'Does it speak?'

'Yes, but she's shy. Please don't upset her.'

He headed for the kitchen and Mum sighed. 'You'd better go and rescue her, sweetheart. She'll be terrified of him.'

Far from being terrified, Ceri was blushing and giggling as she stood at the sink with her hands in the water. We could hear the rain drumming on the roof.

'You're beautiful,' he said. 'You're wasted out here in this Godforsaken place. Hasn't anyone told you? You're like a blonde Audrey Hepburn! Get your hands out of that sink and have a glass of wine.'

I had heard of people's faces lighting up, but I never knew what it meant until then. For the first time, Ceri looked pretty and her blue green eyes shone.

There was a loud knocking at the door and Mum opened it. A man came in, stooping under the doorway. He stood awkwardly, looking around at the steamy chaos of our kitchen, and Alistair in his pink silk shirt and spotted bow tie. The man's hair was plastered to his face by the rain and there was mud on his boots.

'Tom Ellis,' he said. 'Come to get Ceri. And I wondered if you'd like a rabbit or two for the pot?'

To my horror, he held out a dangling corpse.

'Thank you,' said Mum. 'Thank you very much. And thank you, Ceri, for all your hard work.' She handed her a ten pound note.

'Thank you, Mrs McCullen.'

Alistair stood in the doorway, watching father and daughter get into their van. 'Enchanting girl,' he said.

'You be careful,' said Mum. 'She's only a baby.'

'Oh, I don't think she is,' said Alistair, using his hands to indicate her curves. 'In fact, I'd say she was rather well developed.'

'What on earth am I to do with that?' said Mum, pointing at the rabbit.

Dad and Alistair laughed.

Ceri was round next day and Mum gave her a pair of rubber gloves and a dustpan and brush. 'Don't throw the broken glass in the yard away,' she said. 'I can use that in a mosaic.'

On Sunday evening, the Buddhists left, but Alistair stayed on. Ceri appeared again in the morning and offered to show us around the area. She led the way through oak woodland to the river bank, and demonstrated her skill in bouncing fragments of slate across the surface of the water. For the first time, she had discarded her dark, baggy clothes for shorts and a grey marl vest, and her slim pale arms gleamed in the soft sunlight as she balanced on the stepping stones. Alistair had brought his camera; when he pointed it at Ceri she screamed and hid her face.

'Don't be shy, kid,' he said. 'You've got a face made for the camera.'

'Stand sideways, like this, Ceri,' I said, 'and look down, like the stars in the magazines.' I put my hands on my hips, thrust my pelvis forwards and bared my teeth as if to display expensive dentistry.

She copied me and quickly got the hang of it. When we arrived back at the farmhouse Alistair took me and Ceri into the barn for more photographs. It was filled with the wheels of old tractors and other pieces of machinery – the original use of which I could only guess at. Mum was planning to turn these rusty bones into sculpture, but for now they were the backdrop to our poses, along with collapsing shelves, cobwebby beams, and a three legged wooden chair.

Mum brought out wine and lemonade and we sat on a bench in the yard. 'It's so beautiful here,' said Mum, and for the first time since we had arrived, I too could see the beauty in the place, as cloud shadows danced across the hilltops. The flaking paint on the window frames and the weeds flourishing in every corner seemed to enhance the beauty of the rough stone walls. 'I'd like to have hens so we can eat fresh eggs,' she said. 'And I could use the old drinking trough to grow herbs and onions. There's a clump of lobelia in that corner, which someone must have planted. Do you remember if the Pughs did much gardening, Ceri?'

Ceri shook her head. 'Don't know why you like it. When I leave Wales I'm never coming back.'

'You stick with me, girl, you'll soon be going places,' said Alistair, with a nod towards his camera. 'I know a star in the making when I see one. Trust your Uncle Alistair.'

'Don't you listen to him, Ceri,' said Mum.

'What's this, Martha?' he said. 'You're not feeling jealous, are you, of these two beautiful girls? It must be hard for a fine looking woman like yourself, when your looks start to fade, just as your daughter starts to blossom.'

Dad looked up from his iPad. 'Watch it, mate,' he said. 'You'll get a slap if you're not careful.'

'You're not threatening to hit your oldest friend, are you?' said Alistair.

'I wouldn't take the trouble myself, but I'm reminding you, Martha can be vicious if you go too far. When she narrows her eyes like that, you need to look out.' He poured himself another glass of wine.

I knew from past experience that the evening was about to

deteriorate, and soon there would be raised voices, swearing, and perhaps even tears. On one occasion, neighbours had called the police, and on another everyone had to go to hospital, where Alistair sobbed out extravagant apologies while waiting for Dad's wounds to be stitched. In the morning, everyone would appear to have forgotten all about it, and would reinvent the evening as a fine time had by all, fully justifying the painful hangovers.

I asked Ceri if she would join me upstairs, but she said something about having to get back to her Dad who would kill her if she was late, so I went to my room alone. We had not got round to re-decorating upstairs and the floral wallpaper chosen by the Pughs was stained by damp and peeling from the walls. There was a sheepskin rug on the bare floorboards and an old blanket at the window kept the moonlight out.

I woke later that night to find Mum making up a camp bed in my room.

'Are you awake?' she whispered. 'Nothing to worry about, but Ceri needs somewhere to sleep. She's had a row with her dad and she doesn't feel safe at home.'

Over a late breakfast next day, while Ceri slept upstairs, Mum said that Ceri's father had hit her.

'She doesn't look particularly battered,' said my father.

'Well, a man like that will be careful not to leave marks.'

'Doesn't she have any other family she can go to?'

'Apparently not. Anyway, I've said she can stay as long as she needs to. You must admit, it's worth it, to see Rowena smile.'

Ceri soon became the friend I had never had, and we shared our favourite daydreams as we walked by the river or lay in bed at night. We would have big houses, full of servants to attend to our every whim, and our parties would be legendary. People who offended us would be invited, and poisoned. Ceri favoured strychnine, but I persuaded her to consider laxatives instead, and we nearly fell out of bed laughing at the thought of it. Sometimes, in our imaginary worlds, we would toy with the affections of a crowd of admirers, but at other times we were inclined to accept an adoring husband and a handful of angelic children. Ceri would have a dog: I preferred a Persian cat and a white stallion.

I showed Ceri how to weave a friendship bracelet from Mum's embroidery threads, and she responded by pulling three hairs from her head and weaving them into one for me. It was in shades of green, like the hills in Mum's unfinished tapestry. Of course I had to pull out some of my own hair to include in a bracelet for Ceri, although my hair was shorter and darker than hers.

On Friday night Ceri whispered to me that she and Alistair had fallen in love. I giggled, then realised that I was laughing alone.

'But he's old!' I cried. 'And he's not handsome a bit. Or rich.'

'None of that matters when you're in love,' she told me. 'He is my soul mate.' She lowered her voice. 'We did it in the barn yesterday. It was lovely.'

Alistair had held me as a baby and tickled my toes. I shut my eyes and put my fingers in my ears. 'No, don't tell me about it!'

I blame myself for what happened next. Mum and Dad were out shopping all day Saturday, and Alistair and Ceri spent most of the day in his bedroom. I heard movements and giggling, and knew that I would not be welcome, so I wandered by the river and watched the sun sparkling on the surface of the water. I could still see the beauty, but as though through a cloud of emotions I could not understand. When I returned they were in the kitchen, dishevelled and barefoot, and Alistair tried to put his arm around me.

'You're not cross with me, Rowena?' he said, his head tilted, his voice soft, like a baby's. 'You look like your mother, when you narrow your eyes like that.' I shrugged his arm off and he said something to Ceri I could not hear.

'Rowena won't tell,' said Ceri. 'We're friends, Ro, aren't we?'

Then we heard the sound of Dad's car, approaching carefully over the rough road and drawing up outside the house. Alistair ran to greet them, like an enthusiastic puppy. 'What have you bought for me? Are there chocolate biscuits in those bags?'

Ceri smiled at me, her finger on her lips, and whispered, 'Not a word.'

I did not say a word, but Mum must have known that something was wrong. She set us all to work, Ceri to peel potatoes, Alistair to make a salad dressing, while I stood at the sink, washing a lettuce. The outer leaves were slimy, nibbled by slugs.

'Oh, how sweet,' Mum said to Alistair. 'Rowena's made you one of her bracelets.' I turned to see the band of blue and green on his arm, with blonde hairs interwoven, and turned back to the sink. The kitchen fell silent, with just the sound of the running tap and Mum's chopping knife.

'Rowena,' said Mum, 'I can see you've been in my room. You know I don't mind you trying on my things, but you could have put them away more tidily.'

'I didn't go in your room,' I said, and then wished I had kept quiet.

'Sorry, Mrs McMullen,' said Ceri. 'It was me. Alistair's been taking some photos of me for the director and I borrowed one of your lovely scarves.'

'What director is this?'

'You know. His film director friend.'

Alistair appeared preoccupied with the contents of the larder, searching for salad dressing ingredients.

'Ceri, it's not going to happen,' said Mum. 'Alistair doesn't have any contacts to help anyone get into films. It's years since he even had a proper job.'

There was a long moment of silence. Ceri looked at Alistair. 'It's not true, is it, Ali?'

He refused to meet her gaze. 'It's true that you're a lovely girl and I'll always treasure the time we've had together. But I may have exaggerated my influence a little.'

'I'm sorry if I've disappointed you, but it's best you know now,' said Mum. 'Acting requires as much hard work as any other job – it's not all prancing about on a red carpet, you know.' She sliced an onion briskly. 'In fact, I think it would be best if you moved on now. I understand you won't want to go back to your father, but couldn't you stay with your mother for a bit?'

I expected an angry outburst – but whatever Ceri was feeling she kept hidden. Her knuckles went white as she gripped the kitchen knife, but then she put it down and said, 'OK. I'll ring my mum now.'

I went after her, wanting to say that Mum had not meant it and that she must stay, but before I could say anything, Ceri said, 'It's all right. I knew that it wasn't for real.' She smiled at me, but the redness round her eyes told another story and I realised that she needed to be alone.

We were sitting down to dinner when Ceri returned and said that she would be leaving us next day. Mum smiled. 'That's lovely. We'll give you a lift to the station.'

'Thank you, Mrs McMullen. May I use the kitchen to make some cakes for our supper? I'd like to say thank you to you all for having me.' Mum said of course, and Ceri insisted on doing all the washing up alone before she passed round a plate of fairy cakes and some mugs of hot chocolate. As Alistair took the sugar topped morsel she offered him, there was something in her eyes which for a moment made me want to snatch the cake away before he swallowed it. But I told myself not to be silly, and held my breath as he ate the cake, crumbs spilling on to his trousers. No painful spasms ensued; we drank our hot chocolate in silence until a sudden snore from Mum made me jump.

'Oh dear, I think I'd better have an early night,' she said.

Ceri and I did not chat that night: I fell asleep as my head hit the pillow. Next morning I woke to see Ceri's bed empty, and felt a chill deep inside. The room was full of daylight, and downstairs someone was shouting. Then I heard Dad's heavy feet on the stairs, the cry of 'Where's my car?' followed by loud swearing. Not only had Dad's car disappeared, but with it our silver candlesticks, Mum's jewellery, Alistair's camera, and all our computers, cash and credit cards. Worst of all, someone had painted 'Wankers' in big black letters across the dragon mural. Ceri's empty bed did not seem at first to be linked.

'What I can't believe,' said Mum to the policeman, 'is that I've lived most of my life in London, and never been burgled, and now this happens within a month of living in Wales.'

'I expect you were more careful about security in London,' said the policemen. 'It doesn't look as though they had to force any locks. Have you noticed any strangers hanging around?'

'We've hardly seen anyone here. Just our neighbours.'

'Neighbours?'

It turned out that almost nothing Ceri told us had been true. She and her boyfriend – for the tall man we had seen was not her father at all – had been sleeping in a camper van after travelling from

Aberystwyth. Their technique was for Ceri to infiltrate a household with a hard luck story, identify what could be stolen and then to disappear. It was not the first time either that she had administered sleeping pills in cocoa, to keep her victims unconscious while she robbed them.

'We'll catch them eventually,' the policeman assured us, 'but I'm afraid you shouldn't expect to get your property back.'

Of the three adults, Alistair was the one who took longest to accept what had happened. After a morning of intermittent ranting and telephone calls, Dad put his arm around Mum, reminded her that our stolen possessions were only things, and even picked up a paintbrush – something I had never seen before – to repair the mural.

But Alistair's sense of outrage went deeper. 'She lied to us,' he kept saying. 'It's all right for you, you'll probably write a screenplay based on it.'

'As a matter of fact, it has given me an idea,' said Dad. 'But you got your leg over, didn't you? Just be grateful her boyfriend wasn't more of a jealous type.'

That conversation ended when they realised I was in the room.

By September we were back in London and Dad had a new car. Mum still tells people about our old farmhouse, and the painting we did on the wall, and how she intends to take up spinning and weaving – but somehow we never find time to go back there. 'It's dull for Rowena,' says Mum. 'Such a lovely place – but you know what teenagers are like.'

I keep the bracelet Ceri – as I still think of her – made me, in a shoe box. I never wear it, but sometimes I get it out and look at it, and wonder if she still has mine.

SECRETS
KATE ELLIS

Mr Probert watches the girls doing PE in their gym knickers.
The Reverend Pryce kissed a lady behind the chapel.
'Look what I've found.'

Bryn was holding some grubby scraps of paper, reading them with a wide, school boy grin on his face. Any excuse to stop work.

'What are they?' Emrys Williams knew they should be getting on with the conversion. That's what they were being paid for. But he was glad of a break.

'See for yourself,' said Bryn, waving the things about as if they were winning lottery tickets.

Emrys had been dismantling the old pulpit, the centre of Sunday attention in those far off days of his childhood. The man who'd bought the chapel, wanted it moved, saying it would make a nice bar. Bryn was grateful for the cash but he couldn't help experiencing a stab of nostalgia as he picked his way across the rubble fallen from the ceiling that once echoed to the sound of five hundred voices singing in harmony. He hadn't discussed his feelings with Bryn, whose passions were confined to sport and boasting about drunken evenings with his mates. Bryn came from a different generation, a generation with no affinity with the place. To Bryn, the graceful white chapel on the edge of the village was just another renovation job.

Bryn handed over his treasure. The scraps of lined paper had ragged edges and looked as if they'd been torn from an old exercise book.

'Where did you find them?' Emrys asked as he began to read.

'Stuffed down the side of one of the pews at the back. I started to take it apart and there they were, hidden in a crack. Looks like kids' writing.' He smirked. 'Kids with dirty minds.'

Emrys stared at the curled scraps and for a few moments he was eight again, no longer a fifty-six-year-old builder with a growing paunch and a bald spot on the crown of his head which turned red when the sun shone.

'You're from Llanperant. Recognise any of the names?'

'Might do.' This was something he didn't want to share with young Bryn with his tattoos and his monkey grin. These were ghosts from his past.

'There are more in there. Want a look?'

Without waiting for an answer, Bryn hurried away to the back of the chapel where he'd begun to take the old pews apart. As Emrys stood watching, he could see the older children huddled in the back pews, passing scribbled notes to each other during the Minister's interminable sermons. Sharing secrets. And someone must have stuffed some of those secrets down a gap in the wood instead of pocketing them to take home and throw on the coal fire when the parents weren't looking. Emrys was three years younger than the others so he'd been on the fringe of that group, excluded from the game. His big brother, Huw, the popular and outgoing one, had treated him like a nuisance. But Huw had drunk himself to death ten years ago.

Bryn returned with another handful of notes, folded small like the others. With growing impatience, Emrys watched as he unfolded and read them. If anyone had a right to read them first, it was him. He'd been there.

'That Mr Probert must have been an old pervert. Do you remember him?'

'He taught maths at the high school.'

'These days he'd be locked up.'

'He had some sort of accident if I remember right. Let me see those, will you.'

But Bryn ignored him and began to read out loud. '*Nerys Jones snogged with Billy Richards. Jimmy Gough touched Gwyneth Davis's tits at the playground. Matthew Johns told a lie to Mr Probert.* Know what I think?'

'I'm not bloody clairvoyant.'

'I think it was a game – like consequences. Did you play it?'

'I was too young. They wouldn't let me.'

'Who wouldn't?'

'My brother and his mates. Let's get back to work. There's a lot to do.'

But Bryn pretended he hadn't heard and unfolded another note. '*David Bell cheated in his maths test.* Did you know David Bell?'

'Does it matter?' Emrys turned away. The mention of David Bell's name had awakened a memory. Something unpleasant that had lain dormant until that moment.

'What is it? What did he do, this David Bell?'

Emrys knew Bryn wasn't going to give up until he got an answer. 'He went missing one afternoon after school. Never seen again.'

Bryn's eyes lit up with curiosity. 'What do you think happened to him?'

'I've no idea. People went out to look for him but...'

Bryn took another note from the pocket of his stained jeans.

'Listen to this one. *I saw Nerys Jones and Huw Williams being horrid to David Bell and they told me not to tell.* What do you make of that?'

Emrys felt his face burning at the mention of his brother's name. He opened his mouth to answer but no sound came out.

Bryn carried on. 'Here's another. *Myfanwy Pryce saw David Bell talking to Mr Probert but she never told the policeman.'*

'That's enough. Come on. They want this place ready before Christmas.'

Myfanwy Pryce. Emrys remembered the plump Minister's daughter with her freckles and the mousy hair she always wore in plaits. He still saw her from time to time, just in passing to say hello. She'd joined the police and become a senior detective but she'd never married. And she'd stayed in Llanperant to look after her father when he developed dementia. He wondered whether she'd retired. But now her dad was dead, what else would she have in her life apart from work?

He wondered if she'd ever revealed her secret about David Bell and Mr Probert. Or had the secrets just been made up by kids with over-active imaginations to while away the time while the Reverend Pryce held forth about sin and redemption from the pulpit that would soon become a bar. He'd turn in his grave if he knew.

Bryn interrupted his thoughts. 'Look at this one.' He was reading another scrap, devouring the words greedily. *'I know where David Bell is.* What do you make of that?'

Myfanwy Pryce had changed nothing in the house since her father passed away. She wasn't sure whether this was out of respect for his memory or out of idleness. But she suspected the latter.

Every room held memories of him. He'd been a kindly man, a godly man, but she'd always feared that she'd let him down in some unspecified way. She'd felt that way since she'd messed around in chapel with those other kids, trying her hardest to be one of them instead of the Minister's daughter, set apart by her father's position in the community. Maybe an everlasting sense of inadequacy was the price she'd had to pay for living with a saint.

He'd encouraged her in her career, greeting each of her promotions with genuine pleasure. During his lengthy last illness she'd used work as a distraction from the unfolding tragedy of his decaying mind. When she'd made it to Detective Inspector, he hadn't understood. He'd asked if she'd be working on the same ward as Biddy. Her Aunt Biddy had been a nurse... and she'd died twenty five years before.

Myfanwy switched on the TV. Things were quiet at work so she'd left earlier than usual that evening. There had been a spate of robberies from local farms but an arrest had been made that morning. The others had seemed pleased to get home but, having nobody to go home to, she had hung around the office, trying to find things to do. It was only when the cleaners arrived that she'd left, picking up a ready meal from the supermarket on the way home.

The TV chattered in the corner, providing spurious company, but she paid little attention to the screen as she ate off the tray on her knee, shovelling the tasteless mush that claimed to be shepherd's pie into her mouth. She was almost glad when the doorbell rang, although she couldn't think who it would be.

Hers was a detached house; the Minister's house, built by the Victorians with doll's house symmetry. It was far too large for her but she knew she could never move away. In her father's day there were always people at the door and meetings in the front parlour. But since his illness, the house echoed with ghosts.

It took her a couple of seconds to place the man standing on the doorstep. She'd known Emrys Williams's brother, Huw because they'd been in the same class at school. But Emrys himself, being three years younger, had been outside her social sphere.

'Myfanwy. Remember me? Emrys Williams.' The man was smiling

hopefully.

When she invited him in he looked relieved.

'I hear you're working on the chapel.' She couldn't hide the disapproval in her voice; her pain that the centre of her late father's existence was being transformed into another up-market chapel conversion for prosperous townies.

'That's right. How are you, Myfanwy? Don't see much of you in the village these days.'

'I've been busy.' She led him into the living room and turned down the volume on the TV. The meaty odour of her ready meal still hung in the air. The room smelled like their old school canteen.

She sat down but he stood, shifting from foot to foot. She could tell he was nervous. In her job she'd seen a lot of people like that, especially people who were about to make a confession or reveal some sinful secret. 'What can I do for you?' she asked.

He held out a cardboard folder as if he was giving her a quote for some building work. But instead he opened it and passed her a handful of scruffy scraps of paper.

'We found these in the chapel stuffed down one of the back pews.'

As soon as she started to read them she was back there, sitting in the chapel with the other children, ignoring her father's voice thundering from the pulpit. She'd tried so hard to be one of them; to play their games; to make the rudest jokes; to fit in.

'We wrote these during the sermons,' she said. 'You were younger so...'

'My brother, Huw, gets a mention.'

She nodded. 'We called it 'secrets'. Everyone had to write a secret they knew and pass it on. Nerys Jones snogging Billy Richards, eh. She's a local councillor now – on the Police Authority.' She frowned.

'This thing about my da kissing a woman behind the chapel won't be right but I seem to remember that if you didn't know a secret you made one up. Why have you brought them to me?'

Emrys had kept a couple back. Now he handed them to Myfanwy without a word and waited while she read them.

'I thought you'd better see that one,' he said. 'David Bell went missing and... It says you saw David talking to Mr Probert and didn't tell anyone.'

'I remember David going missing but I'm sure I would have told my father if I'd known anything. I was eleven years old – a child.'

'Remember Mr Probert?'

'He used to come here sometimes for meetings.' She paused. 'I can't say I liked him much. But it was a shame about his accident of course,' she added piously.

'Did you know he used to watch the girls?'

Myfanwy shook her head.

'What about that one. *I know where David Bell is.* Recognise the writing?'

She studied it for a few moments. 'It's a long time ago, Emrys.'

'The writer's put little hearts on top of the i's. Must be a girl, don't you think?'

'Nerys Jones used to do that. She got into trouble for it at school.'

'Did she play the secrets game?'

'Oh yes,' she said, recalling that Nerys's secrets were often vicious and usually ficticious. She'd never liked the girl. And, from her rare recent dealings with her, she felt she hadn't improved with age.

'You think she knew something about David Bell's disappearance?'

'We wouldn't reopen an investigation on such flimsy evidence. Besides, most of these so called secrets came from the fevered imagination of a bunch of pre-adolescent kids.'

'What about David Bell's family?'

Myfanwy shrugged. 'He lived in a smallholding a couple of miles outside the village with his mother who wasn't married, which was a big thing in those days in a place like this. As for what happened to her...' She hesitated. 'Why don't you leave those notes with me? I'll see what I can find out.'

'Didn't Mr Probert's accident happen around the time David vanished?'

'That's right. He had a fall and died a few days later, although my father never said much about it, which was unusual when someone in the village passed away.'

'I'd better go. Wife's expecting me back.'

As she stood up to show him out she looked a little disappointed.

'Emrys,' she said when he'd opened the front door. 'I'm sorry about Huw.'

'It was a long time ago,' he said quickly.

'Like David Bell's disappearance,' Myfanwy answered.

She watched as Emrys returned to his bulky off road vehicle. This time maybe she could do something.

I know where David Bell is.

Although Myfanwy hadn't said as much to Emrys, the statement intrigued her. She'd been a child when David disappeared and the grown-ups had only spoken of the matter in whispers. Not in front of the children. Even the chapel kids with their secrets game had lived in ignorance of the truth.

Her own memories were hazy. She recalled that David had left school to walk home alone, never to be seen again. The people of

Llanperant had gathered at her house before going out to search and the hunt had eventually fizzled out like a damp firework. There had been no sign of David: it was as if he'd been swallowed by the hilly landscape on his way home from school; returned to nature like a decaying small animal.

After a couple of days the whole affair was never spoken of again and it was as if David had vanished off the face of the earth – as did his mother. The village women hadn't fussed round as they usually did. But then Miss Bell had been an outsider; an English incomer and an unmarried mother. As far as she knew even her parents hadn't offered her their support, which made her feel a little ashamed.

She went into work early the next day and asked a young DC to see if he could find anything about David Bell in the archives. Records from almost fifty years ago weren't computerised so they'd be buried deep in the bowels of the police station, long forgotten and virtually impossible to locate without a considerable effort. He went off mumbling something about it being filthy down there. Myfanwy watched him go, wondering if she was wasting her time. The case was long dead. It was almost as if it had been dead from the start.

She went into her office and took the note from her handbag. Confronting Nerys Jones – now Councillor Mrs Rogers – might be embarrassing. But the problem of David Bell was buzzing in her head now and she knew it wouldn't go away until she'd discovered the truth.

She made a phone call. Councillor Mrs Rogers had a meeting later that afternoon but she was now at home and if DI Pryce wanted to speak to her, she was free for an hour. She was always happy to co-operate with the police.

As Myfanwy drove to Nerys's large detached house on the edge of

Fishguard, she wondered how the Councillor would react to her visit. Not everyone likes to have their pomposity pricked by a reminder of youthful folly.

Councillor Mrs Nerys Rogers was a tall woman with a well-coiffed helmet of brass-blond hair. She wore a pale blue dress of expensive simplicity and welcomed Myfanwy in her badly cut supermarket mac, like a lady of the manor greeting an upper servant.

Myfanwy, remembering her as a spiteful child in pigtails, refused to be intimidated as she handed her the note. 'Did you write this?'

In spite of Nerys's thick foundation, Myfanwy saw the colour drain from her face. 'Where did you get it?'

'Bethesda chapel's being converted into a house. The builder found it and brought it to me. Remember Emrys Williams?'

'I remember his brother, Huw, better. Tragic what happened to him.'

'Did you write it?'

'I can't remember.'

'Another note says that you and Huw were bullying David Bell. You remember David?'

'Yes.' The word was cautious.

'Did you bully him?'

She turned her head away. 'We were kids.'

'He disappeared. Any idea what happened to him?'

The woman blustered for a few seconds. 'Of course not. These notes mean nothing. It was a game. Half our so called secrets were made up.' She paused. 'Why are you wasting time asking these questions?'

She looked worried, as if she was anticipating trouble. Myfanwy did nothing to reassure her.

'What were you and Huw saying to David?'

'How do you expect me to remember after all this time?'

'Try.'

'I think it was something about his mother and one of the teachers. I can't remember. Like I said, it was probably something we made up.'

'To hurt him?'

She didn't answer.

'Are you sure you don't know anything about his disappearance?'

'I only know what my parents said.'

'What was that?'

'They thought the mother had killed the boy and run off. They used to say she was unstable.'

'Are your parents still alive?' The question sounded blunter than she'd intended but it couldn't be helped.

'No. You know how it is. A generation dies off and the memories die with it.'

Myfanwy nodded. She knew alright. Her parents' contemporaries in Llanperant were either dead or had moved far away to be near grown up children.

'What do you think happened to David?'

There was a long silence before Nerys replied. 'His mother left very soon after he disappeared, I know that much because my uncle owned the cottage she was renting. I think my parents were probably right. She killed him and there was some sort of cover up. Perhaps she was mentally ill or...'

Myfanwy knew that, if Nerys's theory was correct, there was bound to be some record of it. It was just a matter of finding it.

'A lot of the secrets seem to be about Mr Probert.'

Nerys raised her eyebrows. 'Surely you remember what he was like,

Myfanwy.'

'I was the Minister's daughter so a lot of things were kept from me.'

Nerys smiled. 'That's true. You were a real little goody two shoes.'

'I wasn't.'

'Whenever you were with us, we could never forget your da standing up in the pulpit spouting sin and damnation at us. You were guilty by association, I'm afraid.'

'Tell me about Mr Probert.'

'There were all sorts of rumours about women going to his house.' She lowered her voice. 'And one of the boys said he touched him once when he was told to stay after school.'

'Was it true?'

Nerys ignored the question and carried on. 'These days he'd probably end up in prison – historic child abuse. Maybe it's a good job he died when he did.'

'Do you remember if he had any dealings with David Bell?'

'David was in his class.' She thought for a few moments. 'Yes, I remember now. Probert was always picking on him, asking to see him after school.'

'And nobody said anything?'

'They were different times, Myfanwy. Secrets were swept under the carpet.' She looked at her watch. 'Look, I've enjoyed this trip down memory lane but I really have things to do.'

'Before I go, was it you who saw my father kissing a woman behind the chapel?'

Nerys began to laugh. 'Worrying you, is it?'

'I'd like to know, that's all.'

'The woman was your mother.' Nerys was laughing at her, just as she had all those years ago, and she felt a sudden wave of anger.

'Maybe you should look into Probert's accident,' Nerys said as she was showing her out. 'What if Probert killed David and hid his body then David's mum went looking for him and pushed him down the stairs?'

Myfanwy took her leave, feeling stubborn resistance to anything Nerys suggested. She'd make her own enquiries.

On her way back to the police station, Myfanwy passed the small, run down cottage where David Bell had lived with his mother. She remembered the boy as friendless and vulnerable; an outsider like herself. She knew she should have befriended him but she'd been so anxious to fit in that she'd shunned him as the others had. They'd looked for him but, as far as she could recall, that search had soon been abandoned. She wondered whether they'd have been more assiduous if the child had been one of their own.

She returned to the police station to find that there was still no sign of any files concerning the David Bell case so, after requesting the records of Probert's accident, she said she had a headache and was going home early.

But she didn't go straight home. When she reached Llanperant she parked the car by the chapel. Emrys Williams' van was still there so she decided to wander inside. She stood in the vestibule, looking in at the chapel through the open oak doors. She'd expected to feel something, nostalgia for her lost childhood or grief at her father's passing, but the devastation she saw was so complete that all she felt was emptiness.

As she stepped into the main chapel she saw Emrys up a ladder. As soon as he spotted her he climbed down, greeting her as if he was glad of her company.

'I went to see Nerys Jones,' she began. 'Or should I say Councillor Mrs Rogers?'

'You didn't mention her fling with Billy Richards, did you?'

'Credit me with some tact. I just wanted to ask you if you ever heard rumours about Mr Probert liking young boys.'

'I remember my brother Huw telling me to steer clear of him when I went to the high school. But it might just have been one of those things kids say.'

'Found any more notes?'

'The lad found a few but I haven't had time to read them yet.' He pointed to a pew in the corner covered with dust and scraps of old paper. 'Help yourself.'

Emrys watched while she read. Most of them were the usual manufactured scandals; entertainments to counteract the dullness of her father's sermons. Then one caught her eye.

'The Minister saw Mr Probert talking to David Bell and he shouted at him.' She read.

'Who shouted?' said Emrys. 'It's ambiguous.'

Myfanwy didn't reply. She was onto the next note. She stared at it for a few moments before stuffing it in her pocket. 'Thanks for showing me these, Emrys. Sorry, I've got to go.'

'You're not going to reopen the case of David's disappearance, are you?'

'I don't know.' She didn't want to give too much away. There was something she hadn't felt up to facing; something she'd pushed into the attic, out of sight and far from her mind. She knew it would bring her pain but she had no choice.

Myfanwy hadn't been in the loft since she'd deposited her father's papers up there after his death. Those erudite sermons which had so bored her as a child; the perceptive writings he'd always intended to publish somewhere; the extensive notes he'd made on the lives of his flock in order to keep some sort of record of who needed help with what. There were boxes of them, all neatly labelled, and she hadn't been able to face the reminders of what he'd been before the dementia destroyed his mind. All that goodness, all that knowledge and intelligence, gone leaving an empty shell behind.

She hooked down the loft ladder and began to climb the steps. At the station they were still looking for the files on David Bell's disappearance but there was a chance there'd be some mention of it amongst her father's things.

The note she'd taken from the chapel earlier had shaken her. *I saw the Minister with David Bell after school on the day he disappeared.*

She heard her phone ring and sighed as she looked upwards at the black square above her, the open trapdoor that might hold the answer.

When she answered her phone she was surprised to hear the voice of her second in command.

'How are you feeling, guv?' he asked. But Myfanwy sensed that he hadn't called just to enquire about her health.

'Just a headache. I'll be in tomorrow. Everything okay there?'

'Fine apart from a break-in at a chippy in Haverfordwest. Fortunately nobody got battered.'

For the first time Myfanwy was grateful for his appalling sense of humour. The feeble joke had made her smile for the first time that day.

'I'm just ringing to say we've had some luck with that case you've been asking about. We haven't found any mention of the kid's disappearance yet but we have got a report on the death of that teacher. Trefor Probert. The coroner ruled that his death was accidental. He fell down his cellar steps and went into a coma; died two days later without regaining consciousness. We also found something interesting on the missing lad's mother. When did you say he disappeared?'

'Must have been April 1966.'

'Well shortly afterwards she moves from Llanperant to Cardiff and changes her name by deed poll from Yvonne Bell to Yvonne Ogden-Bull. Then a couple of months later she vanishes from the record completely. She might have gone abroad but it strikes me as being an odd thing to do if your kid's missing.'

'Very odd,' said Myfanwy. She put down the receiver and made her way back upstairs, taking in the information. She paused at the foot of the steps before climbing up into the darkness and when she flicked on the loft light she was confronted with the boxes that contained her father's life.

It was an hour before she found what she was looking for – the large notebook, black as the old Bible on the chapel lectern, in which her father had written things he'd never shared with anyone else. She began to read and when she'd finished she sat on the cold loft floor and cried.

The next morning DI Myfanwy Pryce arrived at work early. She had an announcement to make. A cold case had been solved – or rather it had never really been a case, not according to the police at the time.

She called for attention and scanned the sea of curious faces. She was about to talk about another world. A time fifty years ago when children obeyed without question and their little rebellions were kept secret, passed around when nobody was looking in the reverent hush of Sunday chapel. It was inevitable that some betrayed the trust placed in them. And so it was with Trefor Probert.

Her father's notebook, his private record of the community's darkest sins, had told her everything she needed to know.

After a few moments she spoke, breaking the expectant silence. 'As most of you will know, I've been trying to find the file on a child who went missing in Llanperant in 1966.' She paused. 'As yet there's no file but I have made some interesting discoveries.'

A murmur went round the room. 'Are we going to make an arrest, ma'am?' someone asked.

Myfanwy ignored the question. 'Let me take you back to 1966,' she began. 'A child, an English incomer with few friends and a single mother, goes missing on his way home from school. There's a search but it doesn't last long. Why? Because my father, the Minister in the village at the time, discovered the truth behind the disappearance. Listen.' She took out her father's black notebook and began to read.

'Miss Bell turned up at the house in a distressed state and made me promise that what she told me would go no further. Naturally I agreed, saying that it wasn't my place to betray my congregation's secrets. Not that she was really one of my congregation but I felt bound to treat her as if she was. She told me that her son, David hadn't come home from school. She'd panicked and reported it to the police and some people from the village were out looking for him. But now she'd had time to think about it she knew where he might be. I told her she should tell the police but she said it was better if they weren't involved. If we found him she'd tell them it was a false alarm.'

She paused and looked around the room. Her colleagues were

sitting in silence, waiting for her to carry on.

'I immediately went with her without informing my wife what I was doing. She led me to a cave in the hillside outside the village where, she said, the boy spent a lot of time alone and, sure enough, we found him there, cowering and shaking with shock. I did my utmost to help, talking to the boy gently, persuading him to go home. Then, in sobs, he told his story. He had gone to the home of a man who began to do things he knew were wrong and, in his desperation to escape, he'd pushed the man through an open cellar door. The man lost his footing and fell down a flight of steps and when the boy saw he wasn't moving he assumed he was dead. He had killed a man and he named his victim as his teacher, Mr Probert. I was aware of rumours that Probert was involved with a woman, although nobody knew her identity, but I never for one moment thought him capable of such wickedness. For there are none so wicked as those who would corrupt the innocent. I returned with David and his mother to their cottage and told them to stay there until I decided on the best course of action.'

She took a deep breath before continuing.

'It wasn't until mother and son were safely away from the village that I informed the police that David had been found safe, saying that Miss Bell had contacted me to say that her son had come home after having hidden in a disused outhouse because he'd been upset by the way some of the other children treated him at school. I said they had decided to move away to relatives in the city and didn't wish any further action to be taken on the matter. Nobody ever connected the boy's disappearance with Probert's death, which was taken for an accident, so all was well. I trust that the boy will recover from his ordeal...and I pray that I have done the right thing. However, I have been party to a terrible deception and there are times when my conscience troubles me greatly.'

When she stopped reading she looked up. 'Anyone up for tracing this lad and trying to press charges?'

Sensing the challenge in her voice, everyone shook their heads.

'How many of us would blame a pervert's victim for fighting back?' someone said. Myfanwy saw nods of agreement. It was over. Case closed.

The new owner of Bethesda chapel thought it was about time he found out how the work was progressing. He had bought it at auction after returning to Wales from France where he'd lived most of his life.

He had known the chapel many years ago and still held the mental picture in his head. However, it was his memories of the beautiful countryside surrounding the village that fuelled his desire to return to Llanperant.

When he'd discovered that little cave on the hillside, the countryside had become his refuge all those years ago. Hiding there, he'd kept an eye on the village and he'd felt all powerful as he watched its inhabitants. They'd looked like small, harmless models from that distance. It was only when you went near them that they became dangerous.

But almost half a century had passed since then. Even if some of his old school contemporaries still lived in the village, he was sure he'd never be recognised; not after the ravages of time and his change of name.

While his mother was alive he'd never have contemplated returning because he'd had to protect her from the consequences of her passions. When he'd caught her arguing with Mr Probert that day he'd tried to hold her back but she'd been out of control. Later he'd learned that they'd been lovers and that Probert had betrayed her with someone else...but, in his youthful innocence, he'd had no idea of that at the time. Mr Probert had been kind to him, singling him out for special tuition, so he'd been horrified when he'd seen his mother lose control and push him down the steps into the cellar.

If anyone had discovered the truth, they'd have taken his mother away from him so he'd lied to the Minister. He'd lied about Mr Probert, saying he'd made him do terrible things, and he'd claimed he'd killed him in self defence before running away. He'd been good at lying back then.

His mother had been frantic with worry when he'd run off to the cave, but he'd needed time to think of the best way to save her from her own volatile nature. To save them both.

The Reverend Pryce, full of righteous anger, had been all too ready to believe his story and his sympathetic silence had allowed him and his mother to leave the village without alerting the authorities. The Minister had kept their secret...or what he imagined was their secret.

But now his mother was gone, none of that mattered any more.

He pushed open the chapel door and looked round. The partitions were up, forming rooms where the congregation had once sang hymns and listened to the Reverend Pryce preaching, his musical voice reverberating from the sky blue ceiling that had always reminded him of the heavens. Perhaps he'd paint it that colour again. Perhaps.

The builder was still there, messing with an electric drill. They had only communicated by phone and e-mail but now they were face to face he looked vaguely familiar.

'Hello.'

The builder looked up, surprised at the interruption.

'We haven't met before. I'm David Ogden-Bull. I own this place.'

WEEPING QUEENS

CHRISTINE POULSON

Every morning someone went down to the beach ahead of me. There were fresh footprints along the gully between the banks of marram grass, going and coming back. When they reached the beach, they disappeared in the soft sand that was constantly ruffled by the wind sweeping in from the Atlantic.

Every day I went down a little earlier, hoping to catch a glimpse of my unseen companion.

And then the day came when the footprints went out and didn't come back...

But I'm getting ahead of myself. The story begins earlier than that, though how much earlier, who can say? Decades, certainly, maybe longer. But I'll start with the day I left London and drove west into Wales.

I'd told my friends that I needed to be alone to work on my book on the Arthurian legends in Wales. There were photos I needed to take, chapters I needed to outline. That was the truth, but not the whole truth.

Yes, I packed a box of books, planned an itinerary of visits to the most important sites, but also into the car went chocolate, wine, DVDs – everything I could think of that might distract me and soothe a broken heart. He was married. I'd been a fool, had believed him when he said his marriage was over. But I wasn't enough of a fool as to stick around when at last I realised that nothing was going to change. I was half-sick, perhaps a little crazy. Maybe that explains what happened, or some of it at least.

I stopped off near Cardiff to visit Dinas Powys Hill Fort, one of several places put forward as the site of Arthur's court, and it was late afternoon when I arrived at the cottage on the Pembrokeshire coast.

It was a small whitewashed stone building, downstairs a combined sitting room and kitchen with a wood-burning stove and upstairs just one bedroom with twin beds. My sister Pippa would be sharing that with me at the weekend.

The beach was less than ten minutes walk away and I was filled with a childish desire to rush out there straightaway.

I heard the crashing of the breakers before I saw the sea. As I emerged from the gully between the dunes the force of the wind and the gin-cold air took my breath away. The sands stretched out for at least half a kilometre on either side. On this February afternoon they were deserted. It was a dangerous place to swim. A wicked rip current could carry the unwary out to sea. On the other hand it had the reputation of being one of the best surfing beaches in the world and I could well believe it. The waves that were racing in had to be two or even three metres high.

The sun was setting into the sea behind banked up clouds. As I gazed at them, they seemed to take on the shape of an island. I saw hills and trees and little coves rimmed with golden light. I thought of Arthur and his departure for the Isle of Avalon. The Isles of the Blessed, the Fortunate Isles, Tir na nÓg: those mystical portals to the other world were always thought to be in the west, beyond the setting sun. The sun disappeared, the island was just a cloud, and I shivered from the cold.

As I turned to walk up the beach, I saw that I wasn't alone after all. Far off in the distance there was a figure walking northward. Hard to be sure at this distance, but I thought it was a man. Maybe he belonged to the small farmhouse that I could see just inland from the north end of the bay, the windows glowing with a yellow light in the gathering dusk. I'd come here to spend time alone and lick my wounds, but it was comforting to know that there was someone not too far away

I made my way back to the cottage, I unpacked the bags of food that I had brought, and cooked myself the first decent meal I'd had in days. Already I felt at home. London and my faithless lover seemed another world.

Over the next few days I immersed myself in work. I hardly saw a soul. There was still someone in the little farm along the coast, because sometimes there was smoke from the chimney and lights at night, but I didn't see anyone there when I walked past it.

On Friday afternoon my sister Pippa arrived along with Maudie, her black Standard poodle. Pippa and I have always got on. She's the elder, but only by eighteen months, and perhaps because we are so different, we've never been rivals. She's a vet, practical and energetic, not at all fey or prone to imagine things.

After a cup of tea, she took Maudie out for a walk, while I got on with the dinner.

She came back with her face glowing. 'You'll never guess what!'

I looked up from peeling potatoes.

Pippa pulled out a chair and sat down at the kitchen table. 'You know that house further along the bay? Well, I was just going past when Maudie got a scent of something and dashed off round the side of the house. She didn't come back when I called her. When I went to look for her there was a man – he'd been chopping wood – and he was stroking Maudie, pulling her ears. You'll never guess who it was!'

Pippa does likes to eke out a story for maximum effect.

'I don't suppose I will! Just tell me!'

'Only George Windrath!'

'No!'

'Yes!'

I put down the peeler, the potatoes forgotten. George Windrath... wow...

'You're sure?'

She made a face: of course she was sure. Who could fail to recognise the darling of the paparazzi? His was a classic story: humble origins, separated from his family early on and taken into care, reaching rock bottom as a teenage tearaway, rescued by foster-parents to whom he was devoted. He had made a fortune from his software company and endowed a charitable foundation. And more: he was heart-stoppingly handsome. He'd never married or had children, but ex-girlfriends never had a bad word to say about him. A sportsman, too, with a string of racehorses and a passion for four-in-hand carriage competitions...

Pippa's eyes were dreamy. 'I was gobsmacked. I started apologizing. He smiled and said, 'fine dog' and all the time he was stroking Maudie. And then he said, 'I come over here sometimes when I want to be completely on my own.' And I said, I'm not sure exactly what I said, but I wanted him to know that I'd respect his privacy.'

'I'm sure I've read that he's got a house in Pembrokeshire. I'm going to look on my iPad.'

I found an aerial shot of Windrath's house. It was huge: walled garden, stables, the lot, a couple of miles away as the crow flies, quite a bit further by road. It was just one of several: a house in London, a flat in a palazzo in Venice, an apartment in New York overlooking Central Park.

A few more clicks and I brought up a recent photograph of Windrath in Venice with a group of friends.

We gazed at it.

Pippa sighed. 'He's even more gorgeous in real life. He must be forty-five at least, but my God he's hot.'

We shouldn't have opened that second bottle of wine. I always sleep badly when I've had too much to drink. I don't know what I dreamed, but I must have been talking in my sleep, because I felt a hand on my shoulder and heard Pippa's voice.

'Ellie, are you alright? Shove up.' She got in beside me, just as she used to do all those years ago when we shared a bedroom. 'Hey, sweetie, you've been crying. The bastard's not worth it...'

'No, no, it wasn't about him. At least I don't think it was. I don't know what it was about.'

Neither of us was a slip of a girl any more and it was a bit of a squash with Pippa jammed up against my side, but comforting too. She soon fell asleep. I moved over to her bed and dropped off myself for a while. It was six thirty when I woke up again, and I knew I wouldn't get back to sleep. I decided to take Maudie for a walk. Maybe if I got down the beach as soon as it was light, I might at last see who was going down there every day. And what if it was George? I couldn't help feeling a bit star-struck. It's natural, isn't it, to want to know what someone famous is like in the flesh?

Dawn was streaking the sky as I made my way down the track to the beach, Maudie padding along beside me. This time the footsteps were going only one way. Ah-ha, I thought, and quickened my pace.

On either side the beach swept away with no one in sight. Maudie whined and ran forward. What I had taken for seaweed or a rocky outcrop was someone lying on the sand. I began to run, my feet sinking in the soft sand. The dog got there first and circled the body, whimpering.

I reached the firmer sand below the line of the tide and then I was kneeling beside him. For a moment I thought it was George Windrath, but no, it was a much younger man, not much more than a boy. He was in a wetsuit, lying on his stomach, his face to one side, pressed into the sand. His eyes were almost closed with a slit of white showing. When I put my hand on his cheek it was cold and clammy.

Had the sea washed him up? But he wasn't wet. And neither was the sand. The tide wasn't going out, it was coming in.

I thought of CPR. I put both hands on his shoulder and pushed. He flopped onto his back and I gasped. There was a gash in his wetsuit and blood had seeped out. I took hold of his wrist and felt for a pulse. I couldn't find one.

I fumbled in my pockets, searching for my mobile. Through my mind flashed an image of it on the kitchen counter where I'd left it to charge.

I stood up and looked around. Not a soul was in sight.

I didn't want to move him before the emergency services arrived in case I injured him further – though really I was sure he was dead. The tide was only half way up the beach and I'd be back with Pippa long before it reached him.

I staggered up the beach through the soft, yielding sand, Maudie bounding ahead of me. It was like those dreams in which you're desperate to get somewhere and can make no progress. I fell over more than once.

Back at the cottage I rang the emergency services and woke up Pippa.

She pulled on some clothes and we ran to the beach. How long had I gone? Twenty minutes? Yet when Pippa and I emerged onto the beach there was nothing there. The body had gone.

'Where is he?' Pippa asked.

I couldn't believe my eyes. 'What's happened? He was over there.'

We went down the beach to the spot where he had been lying. There were bloodstains on the sand.

'Perhaps he got up and walked away. Are you sure he was dead?' Pippa asked.

'He didn't have a pulse!'

'Could the tide have taken him? It can come in very fast, can't it? In Morecambe Bay, doesn't it come in faster than people can run?'

'The tide hasn't got this far yet. It's still coming in. And it's nowhere near as fast as it is in Morecambe Bay.'

'Let's see if Maudie can find him. You know poodles were breed as water dogs? Tracking's in their genes.'

She directed Maudie to the patch of blood and let her sniff it.

'Find, girl,' she instructed her.

Maudie quested around and headed down the beach towards the sea.

We saw that there were marks on the sand, as though the young man had crawled down the beach – or perhaps been dragged to the edge of the water.

Pippa took Maudie back up the beach and encouraged her to pick up a trail in the direction of the dunes. She wasn't interested. As soon as Pippa released her, she dashed back to the water and waded out, whining, before circling back to us.

The water was shallow close to the shore, but further out huge breakers reared up and came crashing down.

Pippa and I looked at each other.

'Well,' she said, 'however he got away, it wasn't by boat.'

Over cups of tea in the kitchen, the police suggested that I'd been mistaken in thinking that the man was dead. He had collapsed, just fainted probably, but had recovered and departed. The blood and the gash were probably the result of an injury from a submerged rock while surfing and could account for the faint. As for the pulse, or lack of one, it wasn't surprising that I hadn't been able to find one, cold and frightened as I'd been.

'What about the scuff marks in the sand?' I asked.

Pippa had taken a photograph on her phone and it was as well she did. The tide had come in fast, and by the time the police had arrived, there was no other evidence of what I had seen.

The two men looked at each other without speaking. I guessed what they were thinking. Dazed and disorientated, possibly concussed, the young man could have crawled the wrong way and ended up in the water.

The younger man said, 'We'll have to see what the next high tide brings.'

The elder of the two, solid, avuncular, saw the expression on my face and quickly added that more than likely, while I was going for help, the surfer had recovered sufficiently to depart under his own steam. They had made a thorough search and he certainly wasn't lying somewhere in the dunes. They didn't lay much store on the dog not finding a trail.

After they'd gone, Pippa said, 'Do you think that's what happened? That he recovered and went away?'

I shook my head, thinking of his face, the half-open eyes.

'He was dead.'

To her credit, she didn't argue with me. All she said was, 'The alternative is that someone took him away.'

'I don't see how they could have done,' I admitted. 'We didn't see footprints or tyre marks. There are one or two footpaths through the dunes, but you couldn't drive along them even in an off-road vehicle. They'd have had to come down this track.'

'We know they didn't do that.'

'There's something else, Pippa. The more I've think about it, the more sure I am that I've seen that boy somewhere before.'

'Around here?'

I shook my head. 'Don't think so.'

'Perhaps it'll come to you. Maybe someone will report him missing and then we'll know who he is.' She drained her tea and stood up. 'Meanwhile there's nothing we can do and there's no point in sitting around, fretting. We were going to go to the lake where Arthur got his sword. Let's get going.'

The three lakes that make up Bosherston Lily Ponds are all connected. They used to open into the sea, but they are now separated from it by a strip of sand. A cold breeze was rippling the dark waters. The woodland setting, the bare trees crowding in, gave the place a secluded, even a sinister, air.

'The Lily Ponds are the Welsh contender for the lake where Arthur receives Excalibur from the lady of the lake,' I told Pippa. 'A hand comes out of the water, flourishing the sword. And at the end, when Arthur lies dying, Sir Bedivere returns it to the same lake. It's a terrible and tragic story.'

'Let's hear it then.'

We set off across the footbridge with a single rail that stretches across the one of the ponds. Maudie followed us, her claws clicking on the wooden slats.

'Well, according to Malory, Arthur has a son, Mordred, by his half-sister, Margawse. He sleeps with her, not knowing who she is. Then later on, Guenevere falls in love with Lancelot. Disaffected knights, including Mordred, force Arthur to acknowledge the queen's adultery. That's treason so she's condemned to death, and she's about to be burned at the stake, when Launcelot rides in and rescues her.'

'Swashbuckling stuff!'

'Indeed. That triggers a civil war and the battle lines are drawn up. By the end of it, Arthur has killed Mordred, but not before Mordred's dealt him a fatal blow.'

'But I thought Arthur didn't die. Isn't he supposed to return at England's hour of need?'

'Opinion's divided about that.' We were halfway across the bridge. I got my copy of Le Morte D'Arthur out of my bag, opened it where I'd marked a page, and leaned against the rail. 'This is what Malory says happened after Bedivere had returned Excalibur to the lake. 'And then Sir Bedivere took the king on his back and so went with him to the water's side... fast by the bank hoved a little barge with many fair ladies in it... and all they had black hoods and all they wept and shrieked.' Arthur asks to be put in the barge and tells Bedivere that they are taking him to the vale of Avalon to be healed of his grievous wound. Bedivere watches the barge until it's out of sight. Later he finds a chapel in the forest where there's a newly dug grave, but can't be certain who is buried there.' Malory concludes: 'Thus of Arthur I find never more written... nor more of the very certainty of his death... but thus was he led away in a ship wherein were three queens."

I'd read it so many times, but I still felt a frisson.

'Oh, wow,' Pippa said, 'and that's supposed to have happened here?'

'Well... of course it's all myth – all legend really. Arthur might have been Welsh, a Celtic chieftain who played a part in holding back the Anglo-Saxon invasions of the late fifth and six centuries. But that's about it. Historians used to think that there was a battle, at which he'd died, but now that's doubtful as well.'

But on that bleak day with the wind rippling the water and the reeds swaying there was something brooding and elemental about the place and it was easy to imagine...

'Hey!' Pippa gripped my arm so tightly that I gasped and nearly dropped my book. I looked up just in time to see something sinking back into the water and ripples spreading out.

Maudie uttered a low, guttural grow.

'What was that?' Pippa demanded.

As we gazed, a snout appeared above the water almost beneath us and we caught a glimpse of a long, dark shape.

'It's a fish, you fathead! A pike. Did you think it was going to be an arm in white samite flourishing a sword?'

Pippa laughed, but she said, 'All the same, there's something about this place... it's as if I've been here before.'

Maudie whined. She'd had enough and wanted to go.

It was only midday, but it was getting dark. Clouds were massing overhead.

'Come on,' I said. 'Let's head for home.'

We had lunch at a pub on the way.

When we got back to the cottage, I went up stairs to lie down.

I soon dropped off and I had the most vivid dream I've ever had. I was hurrying down a dimly lit stone staircase, holding up a long dark skirt. There was a dank smell, the air was clammy. I reached a room, no, not a room, a boathouse. It was dusk. Outside, the sun was setting. Two women were waiting for me. They too were dressed in dark, flowing garments. I couldn't make out their faces. 'Dear sister, you are come,' said one of them and took me by the hand. 'He is waiting.'

There was a barge draped with black cloth. Someone was sitting in it. She turned her face towards me and I saw that it was Pippa, her face tear-stained and haggard. I didn't want to step forward, but it was happening anyway. Someone was lying in the barge, their head on Pippa's lap.

I realised that I was dreaming and that it was King Arthur in the barge. What would he look like, I wondered?

The instant I saw his face, I woke up with a jolt. I found myself sitting up on the bed, my heart thudding.

It had been George Windrath in the boat.

Footsteps came clattering up the wooden stairs and Pippa burst into the room.

'The body on the beach?' she said. 'I know what happened.'

We left Maudie at home this time. As we stepped outside, it seemed to me that the day had changed. It felt as if a storm was coming. The air was already tinged with dusk.

We walked along to the farmhouse. A narrow path led through the dunes to the beach. We followed it.

'That's it, there!' Pippa stopped and leaned forward with her hands on her knees. I saw what she was looking at: a horse's hoof prints.

She went on. 'I hadn't got it quite right about Morecambe Bay.

I looked it up online. The tidal bore doesn't just come in faster than a person can run. It comes in faster than a galloping horse! And I thought – time would be tight, but that's how it could be done.'

'You mean, someone came on horseback through the shallow water? They dragged the body down to the waterline...'

'... and hoisted it onto the horse and galloped back the way they came.'

Pippa straightened up. 'George Windrath breeds Frisians for carriage driving. They're sturdy horses. They were bred in the Middle Ages to carry knights in armour. Windrath must have ridden over on one, maybe yesterday evening. There are stables at the farmhouse.'

She put up a hand to brush something off her hair and frowned. 'What's that?'

I looked up. White and grey flakes were fluttering down from the sky. I couldn't make sense of what I was seeing. Snow? Blossom? I put out a hand and a fragment of burnt paper settled in my palm. Now I could smell it: a fire somewhere near.

A ribbon of blue smoke was unfurling above the dunes.

We followed the path as it climbed and sank between slopes of sand and banks of marram grass until we reached a hollow where a kind of rudimentary hearth had been built of stones. The fire had almost burned down, but bits of charred paper were still rising in its draft. A larger scrap of paper was caught under one of the stones. I reached for it, squinting against the heat.

Only a few lines of the letter remained. With Pippa looking over my shoulder, I read 'my right to be acknowledged... your sister... my mother... I will tell...'

'That's it,' I said. 'That's why he looked familiar. The young man – he must have been George Windrath's son.'

'Come on,' Pippa said.

Her face was stern. I'd never seen her like that before. She almost looked like a stranger.

I followed her and we found ourselves on a rocky outcrop looking down at a seething sea, wilder than I had ever seen it. The dunes had sheltered us and I hadn't realized how much the wind had got up. The setting sun was partly obscured, angry gleams of red shooting through bars of dark grey cloud.

There was a man standing by the edge of the sea, the waves running over his boots.

He turned to look at us. It was George Windrath.

I've since wondered how we must have appeared to him, outlined against the sky, Pippa in her long black coat. Maybe what happened next, would have happened anyway.

I thought he spoke, but if so, it was lost in the thunder of the waves.

He turned back to the sea and walked into the water.

I gasped and would have started forward, but I felt Pippa's hand on my arm.

'No,' she said.

He waded on until he was waist-deep. He leaned into the water and began to swim, breasting the waves, striking westwards towards the setting sun. His head disappeared and reappeared among the surging breakers.

I tasted salt on my lips. Rain was mingling with the tears that were rolling down my face. I looked at Pippa in the fading light and saw that her face was wet, too.

When I looked back, George had gone.

Biographies **Murder Squad**

Photo © Malcom Younger

Ann Cleeves
Author of the Vera Stanhope novels, dramatized by ITV in the TV series *Vera*, starring Brenda Blethyn.
Ann is also the author of the Shetland Island series of books adapted by the BBC into the TV series *Shetland*. The newest book in the Vera series, *The Moth Catcher*, is published by Macmillan in September 2015.

Martin Edwards
Author of *The Golden Age of Murder*, a study of detective fiction between the wars, and of eighteen crime novels, including seven Lake District Mysteries.

Cath Staincliffe
Award-winning author of *Half the World Away*, creator of *Blue Murder* and writer of the Scott and Bailey books.

Chris Simms
Author of a Manchester-based detective series starring DI Spicer, Chris Simms has been nominated for the Theakston's Crime Novel of the Year and Crime Writers' Association Dagger awards for his novels and short stories.

Kate Ellis
Kate Ellis has written many short stories and five Joe Plantaganet crime novels set in York. However, she is best known for her Devon-based series combining past and present crimes and featuring archaeology graduate, DI Wesley Peterson, the latest of which is *The Death Season*.

Margaret Murphy
A Short Story Dagger winner with nine psychological novels published in her own name, and two forensic thrillers written as A.D. Garrett, the latest of which is *Believe No One*.

PEMBROKESHIRE DAVID WILSON

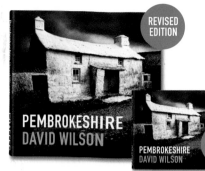

REVISED EDITION

NEW MINI EDITION

'These are powerful images. They remind us that rural Wales has a stark and demanding beauty.' **Griff Rhys Jones**

From the rolling Preseli Hills to its dramatic cliff-top coastline, Pembrokeshire both excites and enthralls with a sense of timeless beauty. And yet there is also a story to be told, one of meaning and of ancestry, which acclaimed landscape photographer David Wilson brings to life through his remarkable black and white images. Join David as he explores his native county through 58 stunning images and discover for yourself what the landscape really looks like.

Pembrokeshire
- Hardback, 120 pages
- Size 300 x 300mm
- ISBN 9781905582921
- Price £30

Mini edition
- Hardback, 120 pages
- Size 150 x 150mm
- ISBN 9781905582938
- Price £9.99

WALES A PHOTOGRAPHER'S JOURNEY DAVID WILSON

A collection of over 150 black and white landscape images by Welsh photographer David Wilson. In this, his second book, David takes the reader on a unique visual journey through Wales. More than just a travelogue, *Wales A Photographer's Journey* is a beautiful collection of photographs which makes both an engaging book and a sumptuous gift.

- Hardback, 160 pages
- Size 300 x 300mm
- ISBN 9781905582594
- Price £35

DAVID WILSON CALENDAR 2016

A full year month-to-view wall calendar which celebrates the work of one of Wales' leading photographic talents. Contains 12 black and white images from around Wales highlighting its architecture and landscape. Images are taken from David's new photography book, *50 Buildings that Built Wales*.

- ISBN 9781909823495
- Price £8.99

Available at bookshops, gifts shops and www.graffeg.com   GRAFFEG

Biographies **Accomplices**

Valerie Laws
Crime novelist, poet, playwright, creator of science poetry installations, and is world-famous for spray-painting poetry on live sheep to celebrate quantum theory.

Helena Edwards
A new author whose first short story, 'If Anything Happens to Me' was recently published in Ellery Queen's Mystery Magazine.

Mary Sharratt
Mary Sharratt is an American who lives in the Pendle region of Lancashire, the setting of her acclaimed novel, *Daughters of the Witching Hill*. Her forthcoming novel, *The Dark Lady's Mask*, based on the dramatic life of Renaissance poet, Aemilia Bassano Lanier, will be published on the 400th anniversary of Shakespeare's death.

Jim Kelly
A former journal Jim wrote his first book, *The Water Clock*, on his London train commute. A past winner of the CWA's Dagger in the Library, Jim is now writing a new seri for Penguin, the Peter Shaw novels.

Christine Poulso
Author of the Cassandra James series of crime novels set in Cambridge. Her most recent book, *Invisible*, a suspense novel, was published by Accent Press in 2014.

Toby Forward
Toby Forward lives in Liverpool. He is the author of over twenty books for adults, young people and children, including the Carnegie Medal nominated *Dragonborn*, the first volume in 'The Flaxfield Quartet'.